PULP *Literature*

BREAK AST
CNIC LUNCH
TOAD
HOLE
25¢
25¢

PULP Literature

PULP LITERATURE PRESS

Issue No. 40, Autumn 2023

Publisher: Pulp Literature Press; Editor-in-Chief: Jennifer Landels; Senior Editor: Mel Anastasiou; Acquisitions Editor: Genevieve Wynand; Poetry Editors: Daniel Cowper & Emily Osborne; Assistant Editors: Brooklynn Hook, Sierra Louie, Ellen Spacey; Copy Editor: Amanda Bidnall; Proofreader: Sierra Louie; Graphic Design: Amanda Bidnall & Sierra Louie; Cover Design: Kate Landels; Subscriptions: Carol McCauley & Brooklynn Hook; Advertising: Brooklynn Hook. For advertising rates, direct inquiries to info@pulpliterature.com.

Cover painting, *American Space Force* by Tais Teng. 'The Drift' by Jordan Bray. All other illustrations by Mel Anastasiou.

Pulp Literature: ISSN 2292-2164 (Print), ISSN 2292-2172 (Digital), Issue No. 40, Autumn 2023.

Pulp Literature Press gratefully acknowledges the support of the Canada Council for the Arts and the Government of Canada.

Pulp Literature is a proud member of the Magazine Association of BC and Magazines Canada.

TABLE OF CONTENTS

FROM THE PULP LIT PULPIT

Here's to the Beer!

As we write this, it's precisely ten years since Mel, Sue, and Jen came up with the crazy idea to launch a fiction magazine. We were sitting on Mel's deck, drinking beer under bold July skies that made anything seem possible … even breaking into genre publishing.

Canada has always had a healthy literary mag scene, but ten years ago, places for genre fiction were few and far between. There were the wonderful *On Spec* and *Neo-opsis*, but both of those were SFF only, while *Mystery Weekly* and *Augur* had yet to start. *Why not*, we thought, *publish all the genres we love in one place?*

We felt it might be pleasant, though, to have some startup money to pay our writers and printers. We pondered for a moment more, and the lightbulb went on. "Kickstarter is a newish crowd-funder south of the border," someone said. "If it ever runs in Canada, we should use it to fund a magazine." We raised our bottles of Innis & Gunn, and drank to that.

Kickstarter opened in Canada the following week.

That same month, bestselling author CC Humphreys and soon-to-be-bestselling author Jen were in rehearsals for a stage combat scene to launch his novel *Shakespeare's Rebel* at Bard on the Beach. One day, as they enjoyed a post-rehearsal bevvy (and yes, beer does seem to play an influential role in the magazine), Jen asked him if he had any shoebox stories, those dusty drafts that sit forgotten under the bed or in the deepest corner of the hard drive. "As a matter of fact," he said, "I do."

And so we acquired our first feature story, 'Where the Angels Wait'. It's reprinted here at the end of our fortieth issue, as a bookend of sorts.

"Wait," we hear you say. "A bookend? Does that mean *Pulp Lit* is ending? Absolutely not! A bookend just means we've reached the end of a ten-year-long shelf and are starting a new one. We've got fabulous pieces from Finnian Burnett, Kelly Robson, Robert Silverberg, David Gerrold, and more lined up for you next year.

But in the meantime, immerse yourself in the final issue of our first decade, starting with a historical SF horror from the estimable Robert J Sawyer. Written in the nineties and set in the early part of this century, it gives us a lens on our future by looking at the past. The horror is visceral, and yet the lens is strangely comforting.

We look forward to providing you many more years of stories that are visceral and comforting, as well as funny, thrilling, complex, and heartwarming. It's one of the pleasures of offering a mosaic of genres, styles, and themes in each issue.

Onwards and upwards, friends!

~ Jen & Mel

In THIS ISSUE

Take a spacewalk into the unknown with *American Space Force* by cover artist **Tais Teng** and feature story 'Above It All' by **Robert J Sawyer**. Dare we look below?

In the next Fairmount Manor mystery by **Mel Anastasiou**, Stella Ryman shows us how to receive the kindness of strangers, while in a new chapter of *The Shepherdess* by **JM Landels**, Toinette needs to accept the help of her foil. And in 'The Lady M' by **Cat Girczyc**, it's not always easy to tell friend from foe.

Explore grief and healing with contest winners that include the Jack Whyte Storyteller Award-winning story by **CZ Tacks** and Magpie Award-winning poetry from **Claire Lawrence, Catherine Lewis**, and **Mark Cameron**.

As courageously as possible, face two final frontiers in work by **Graham J Darling** and **Jordan Bray**, and then return to where it all began with 'Where the Angels Wait' and a bonus start to a new Jack Absolute novel by **CC Humphreys**.

Allaigna's Song

Overture

JM Landels

PULP
Literature

FANTASTIC
FRESH
FICTION

www.pulpliterature.com

ABOVE IT ALL

Robert J Sawyer

Robert J Sawyer *has won both the Hugo and Nebula Awards for best science-fiction novel of the year. The ABC TV series* FlashForward *was based on his novel of the same name. His latest novel is* The Oppenheimer Alternative, *and his next,* The Downloaded, *will be out in May 2024. A member of the Order of Canada, Rob lives in Mississauga.*

$\mathcal{A}$BOVE IT ALL

Rhymes with fear.

The words echoed in Colonel Paul Rackham's head as he floated in *Discovery*'s airlock, the bulky Manned Maneuvering Unit clamped to his back. Air was being pumped out; cold vacuum was forming around him.

Rhymes with fear.

He should have said no, should have let McGovern or one of the others take the spacewalk instead. But Houston had suggested that Rackham do it, and to demur he'd have needed to state a reason.

Just a dead body, he told himself. Nothing to be afraid of.

There was a time when a military man couldn't have avoided seeing death—but Rackham had just been finishing high school during Desert Storm. Sure, as a test pilot, he'd watched colleagues die in crashes, but he'd never actually seen the bodies. And when his mother passed on, she'd had a closed casket. His choice, that, made without hesitation the moment the funeral director had asked him—his father, still in a nursing home, had been in no condition to make the arrangements.

Rackham was wearing liquid-cooling long johns beneath his spacesuit, tubes circulating water around him to remove excess body heat. He shuddered, and the tubes moved in unison, like a hundred serpents writhing.

He checked the barometer, saw that the lock's pressure had dropped below 0.2 psi—just a trace of atmosphere left. He closed his eyes for a moment, trying to calm himself, then reached out a gloved hand and turned the actuator that opened the outer circular hatch. "I'm leaving the airlock," he said. He was wearing the standard 'Snoopy Ears' communications carrier, which covered most of his head beneath the space helmet. Two thin microphones protruded in front of his mouth.

"Copy that, Paul," said McGovern, up in the shuttle's cockpit. "Good luck."

Rackham pushed the left MMU armrest control forward. Puffs of nitrogen propelled him out into the cargo bay. The long space doors that normally formed the bay's roof were already open, and overhead he saw Earth in all its blue-and-white glory. He adjusted his pitch with his right hand control, then began rising up. As soon as he'd cleared the top of the cargo bay, the Russian space station *Mir* was visible, hanging a hundred metres away, a giant metal crucifix. Rackham brought his hand up to cross himself.

"I have *Mir* in sight," he said, fighting to keep his voice calm. "I'm going over."

Rackham remembered when the station had gone up, twenty years ago in 1986. He first saw its name in his hometown newspaper, the Omaha *World Herald*. *Mir*, the Russian word for peace—as if peace had had anything to do with its being built. Reagan had been haemorrhaging money into the Strategic

Defense Initiative back then. If the Cold War turned hot, the high ground would be in orbit.

Even then, even in grade eight, Rackham had been dying to go into space. No price was too much. "Whatever it takes," he'd told Dave—his sometimes friend, sometimes rival—over lunch. "One of these days, I'll be floating right by that damned *Mir*. Give the Russians the finger." He'd pronounced *Mir* as if it rhymed with *sir*.

Dave had looked at him for a moment as if he were crazy. Then, dismissing all of it except the way Paul had spoken, he smiled a patronizing smile and said, "It's *meer*, actually. Rhymes with fear."

Rhymes with fear.

Paul's gaze was still fixed on the giant cross, spikes of sunlight glinting off it. He shut his eyes and let the nitrogen exhaust push against the small of his back, propelling him into the darkness.

"I've got a scalpel," said the voice over the speaker at mission control in Kaliningrad. "I'm going to do it."

Flight controller Dimitri Kovalevsky leaned into his mike. "You're making a mistake, Yuri. You don't want to go through with this." He glanced at the two large wall monitors. The one showing *Mir*'s orbital plot was normal; the other, which usually showed the view inside the space station, was black. "Why don't you turn on your cameras and let us see you?"

The speaker crackled with static. "You know as well as I do that the cameras can't be turned off. That's our way, isn't it? Still—even after the reforms—cameras with no off switches."

"He's probably put bags or gloves over the lenses," said Metchnikoff, the engineer seated at the console next to Kovalevsky's.

"It's not worth it, Yuri," said Kovalevsky into the mike, while nodding acknowledgment at Metchnikoff. "You want to come on home? Climb into the *Soyuz* and come on down. I've got a team here working on the re-entry parameters."

"*Nyet*," said Yuri. "It won't let me leave."

"What won't let you leave?"

"I've got a knife," repeated Yuri, ignoring Kovalevsky's question. "I'm going to do it."

Kovalevsky slammed the mike's off switch. "Dammit, I'm no expert on this. Where's that bloody psychologist?"

"She's on her way," said Pasternak, the scrawny orbital-dynamics officer. "Another fifteen minutes, tops."

Kovalevsky opened the mike again. "Yuri, are you still there?"

No response.

"Yuri?"

"They took the food," said the voice over the radio, sounding even farther away than he really was, "right out of my mouth."

Kovalevsky exhaled noisily. It had been an international embarrassment the first time it happened. Back in 1994, an unmanned *Progress* rocket had been launched to bring food up to the two cosmonauts then aboard *Mir*. But when it docked with the station, those cosmonauts had found its cargo hold empty — looted by ground-support technicians desperate to feed their own starving families. The same thing had happened again just a few weeks ago. This time the thieves had been even more clever — they'd replaced the stolen food with sacks full of dirt to avoid any difference in the rocket's pre-launch weight.

"We got food to you eventually," said Kovalevsky.

"Oh, yes," said Yuri. "We reached in, grabbed the food back — just like we always do."

"I know things haven't been going well," said Kovalevsky, "but—"

"I'm all alone up here," said Yuri. He was quiet for a time, but then he lowered his voice conspiratorially. "Except I discover I'm not alone."

Kovalevsky tried to dissuade the cosmonaut from his delusion. "That's right, Yuri—we're here. We're always here for you. Look down, and you'll see us."

"No," said Yuri. "No—I've done enough of that. It's time. I'm going to do it."

Kovalevsky covered the mike and spoke desperately. "What do I say to him? Suggestions? Anyone? Dammit, what do I say?"

"I'm doing it," said Yuri's voice. There was a grunting sound. "A stream of red globules … floating in the air. Red—that was our colour, wasn't it? What did the Americans call us? The Red Menace. Better dead than Red … But they're no better, really. They wanted it just as badly."

Kovalevsky leaned forward. "Apply pressure to the cut, Yuri. We can still save you. *Come on, Yuri*—you don't want to die! Yuri!"

Up ahead, *Mir* was growing to fill Rackham's view. The vertical shaft of the crucifix consisted of the *Soyuz* that had brought Yuri to the space station sixteen months ago, the multiport docking adapter, the core habitat, and the Kvant-1 science module, with a green *Progress* cargo transport docked to its aft end.

The two arms of the cross stuck out of the docking adapter. To the left was the Kvant-2 biological research centre, which contained the EVA airlock through which Rackham would enter. To the right was the Kristall space-production lab. Kristall had a docking port that a properly equipped American shuttle could hook up to—but *Discovery* wasn't properly equipped; the *Mir* adapter collar was housed aboard *Atlantis*, which wasn't scheduled to fly again for three months.

Rackham's heart continued to race. He wanted to swing around, return to the shuttle. Perhaps he could claim nausea. That was reason enough to abort an EVA; vomiting into a space helmet in zero-g was a sure way to choke to death.

But he couldn't go back. He'd fought to get up here: clawed, competed, cheated, left his parents behind in that nursing home. He'd never married, never had kids, never found time for anything but *this*. He couldn't turn around — not now, not here.

Rackham had to fly around to the Kvant-2's backside to reach the EVA hatch. Doing so gave him a clear view of *Discovery*. He saw it from the rear, its three large and two small engine cones looking back at him like a spider's cluster of eyes.

He cycled through the space station's airlock. The main lights were dark inside the biology module, but some violet-white fluorescents were on over a bed of plants. Shoots were growing in strange circular patterns in the microgravity. Rackham disengaged the Manned Maneuvering Unit and left it floating near the airlock, like a small refrigerator with arms. Just as the Russians had promised, a large pressure bag was clipped to the wall next to Yuri's own empty spacesuit. Rackham wouldn't be able to get the body, now undoubtedly stiff with rigor mortis, into the suit, but it would fit easily into the pressure bag, used for emergency equipment transfers.

Mir's interior was like everything in the Russian space program — rough, metallic, ramshackle, looking more like a Victorian steamworks than space-age technology. Heart thundering in his ears, he pushed his way down Kvant-2's long axis toward the central docking adapter, to which all the other parts of the station were attached.

Countless small objects floated around the cabin. He reached out with his gloved hand and swept a few up in his palm. They were six or seven millimetres across and wrinkled like dried peas. But their colour was a dark rusty brown.

Droplets of dried blood. *Jesus Christ.* Rackham let go of them, but they continued to float in midair in front of him. He used the back of his glove to flick them away, and continued on deeper into the station.

"*Discovery*, this is Houston."

"Rackham here, Houston. Go ahead."

"We — ah — have an errand for you to run."

Rackham chuckled. "Your wish is our command, Houston."

"We've had a request from the Russians. They, ah, ask that you swing by *Mir* for a pickup."

Rackham turned to his right and looked at McGovern, the pilot. McGovern was already consulting a computer display. He gave Rackham a thumbs-up signal.

"Can do," said Rackham into his mike. "What sort of pickup?"

"It's a body."

"Say again, Houston."

"A body. A dead body."

"My God. Was there an accident?"

"No accident, *Discovery*. Yuri Vereshchagin has killed himself."

"Killed …"

"That's right. The Russians can't afford to send another manned mission up to get him." A pause. "Yuri was one of us. Let's bring him back where he belongs."

Rackham squeezed through the docking adapter and made a right turn, heading down into *Mir*'s core habitat. It was dark except for a few glowing LEDs, a shaft of earthlight coming in through one window, and one of sunlight coming in through the other. Rackham found the light switch and turned it on. The interior lit up, revealing beige cylindrical walls. Looking down the module's thirteen-metre length, he could see the main control console, with two strap-in chairs in front of it, storage lockers, the exercise bicycle, the dining table, the closet-like sleeping compartments, and, at the far end, the round door leading into Kvant-1, where Yuri's body was supposedly floating.

He pushed off the wall and headed down the chamber. It widened out near the eating table. He noticed that the ceiling there had writing on it. Rackham looked at the cameras, one fore, one aft, both covered over with spacesuit gloves, and realized that even if they were uncovered, that part of the ceiling was perpetually out of their view. Each person who had visited the station had apparently written his or her name there in bold Magic Marker strokes: Romanenko, Leveykin, Viktorenko, Krikalev, dozens more. Foreign astronauts' names appeared, too, in Chinese characters, and Arabic, and English.

But Yuri Vereshchagin's name was nowhere to be seen. Perhaps the custom was to sign off just before leaving the station. Rackham easily found the Magic Marker, held in place on the bulkhead with Velcro. His Cyrillic wasn't very good—he had to carefully copy certain letters from the samples already on the walls—but he soon had Vereshchagin's name printed neatly across the ceiling.

Rackham thought about writing his own name, too. He touched the marker to the curving metal, but stopped, pulling the pen back, leaving only a black dot where it had made contact.

Vereshchagin's name *should* be here—a reminder that he had existed. Rackham remembered all the old photographs that came to light after the fall of the Soviet Union: the original versions, before those who had fallen out of favour had been airbrushed out. Surely no cosmonaut would ever remove Vereshchagin's name, but there was no need to remind those who might come later that an American had stopped by to bring his body home.

The dried spheres of blood were more numerous in here. They bounced off Rackham's faceplate with little pinging sounds as he continued down the core module through the circular hatch into Kvant-1.

Yuri's body was indeed there, floating in a semi-foetal position. His skin was as white as candle wax, bled dry. He'd obviously rotated slowly as his opened wrist had emptied out—there was a ring of dark brown bloodstains all around the circumference of the science module. Many pieces of equipment also had blood splatters on them, where drops had impacted before they'd desiccated. Rackham could taste his lunch at the back of his throat. He desperately fought it down.

And yet he couldn't take his eyes off Yuri. A corpse, a body without a soul in it. It was mesmerizing, terrifying, revolting. The very face of death.

He'd met Yuri once, in passing, years ago at an IAU conference in Montreal. Rackham had never known anyone before who had committed suicide. How could Yuri have killed himself? Sure, his country was in ruins. But billions of … of rubles had been spent building this station and getting him up here. Didn't he understand how special that made him? How, quite literally, he was above it all?

As he drifted closer, Rackham saw that Yuri's eyes were open. The pupils were dilated to their maximum extent, and a pale grey film had spread over the orbs. Rackham thought that the decent thing to do would be to reach over and close the eyes. His gloves had textured rubber fingertips, to allow as much feedback as possible without compromising his suit's thermal insulation, but even if he could work up the nerve, he didn't trust them for something as delicate as moving eyelids.

His breathing was growing calmer. He was facing death — facing it directly. He regretted, now, not having seen his mother one last time, and —

There was something here. Something else, inside Kvant-1 with him. He grabbed hold of a projection from the bulkhead and wheeled around. He couldn't see it. Couldn't hear any sound conducted through the helmet of his suit. But he felt its presence, knew it was there.

There was no way to get out; Kvant-1's rear docking port was blocked by the *Progress* ferry, and the exit to the core module was blocked by the invisible presence.

Get a grip on yourself, Rackham thought. *There's nothing here.* But there was. He could feel it. "What do you want?" he said, a quaver in his tone.

"Say again, Paul." McGovern's voice, over the headset.

Rackham reached down, switched his suit radio from VOX to OFF. "What do you want?" he said again.

There was no answer. He waved his arms, batting around hundreds of dried drops of blood. They flew all over the cabin — except for an area, up ahead, the size of a man. In that area, they deflected before reaching the walls. Something *was* there — something unseen. Paul's stomach contracted. He felt panic about to overtake him, when —

A hand on his shoulder, barely detectable through the bulky suit.

His heart jumped, and he swung around. He'd been floating backward, moving away from the unseen presence, and had bumped into the corpse. He stopped dead, revolted by the prospect of touching the body again, terrified of moving in the other direction toward whatever was up ahead.

But he had to get out. Somebody else could come back for Yuri. He'd find some way to explain it all later, but for now he had to escape. He grabbed hold of a handle on the wall and pushed off the bulkhead, trying to fly past the presence up ahead. He made it through into the core module. But something cold as space reached out and stopped him directly in front of the small window that looked down on the planet.

Look below, said a voice in Rackham's head. *What do you see?*

He looked outside, saw the planet of his birth. "Africa."

Millions of children starving to death.

Rackham moved his head left and right. "Not my fault."

The view changed, faster than any orbital mechanics would allow. *Look below,* said the voice again. *What do you see?*

"China."

A billion people living without freedom.

"Nothing I can do."

Again, the world spun. *Look below.*

"The west coast of America. There's San Francisco."

The plague is everywhere, but nowhere is it worse than there.

"Someday they'll find a cure."

What else do you see?

"Los Angeles."

The inner city. Slums. Poverty. They haven't abandoned hope, those who live there ... Hope has abandoned them.

"They can get out. They just need help."

Whose help? Where will the money come from?

"I don't know."

Don't you? Look below.

"No."

Look. Your eyes have been closed too long. Open them. What do you see?

"Russia. Ah, now—Russia! Free! We defeated the Evil Empire. We defeated the Communist menace."

The people are starving.

"But they're free."

They have nothing to eat. Twice now they've taken food destined for this station.

"I read about that. Terrible, unthinkable. Like committing murder."

To take food from the mouths of the hungry. It is like committing murder, isn't it?

"Yes. No. No, wait. That's not what I meant."

Isn't it? The people need food.

"No. The space program provides jobs. And don't forget the spinoffs—advanced plastics and pharmaceuticals and ... and ..."

Microwave ovens.

"Yes, and—"

And dehydrated ice cream.

"No, important stuff. Medical equipment. And all kinds of new electronic devices."

That's why you go into space, then? To make life better on Earth?

"Yes. Yes. Exactly."

Look below.

"No. No, dammit, I won't."

Yuri looked below.

"Yuri was a cosmonaut—a Russian. Maybe—maybe Russia shouldn't be spending all this money on space. But I'm an American. My country is rich."

Los Angeles, said the voice that wasn't a voice. *San Francisco. And don't forget New York. Slums, plague, a populace at war with itself.*

Rackham felt his gloved fists clenching. He ground his teeth. "Damn you!"

Or you.

He closed his eyes, tried to think. Any price, he'd said — and now it was time to pay. For the good of everyone, he said — but the road was always paved with good intentions.

Starvation. Enslavement. Poverty. War.

He couldn't go back to *Discovery* — he had no choice in the matter. It wouldn't let him leave. But he'd be damned if he'd end up like Yuri, bait for yet another spacefarer.

He slipped into the control station just below the entrance portal that led from the docking adapter. He looked at the cameras fore and aft, the bulky white gloves covering them like beckoning hands. An ending, yes — and with the coffin closed. He scanned the controls, consulted the onboard computer, made his preparations. He couldn't see the entity, couldn't see its grin — but he knew they both were there.

" — in the hell, Paul?" McGovern's voice, as Rackham turned his suit radio back on. "Why are you firing the ACS jets?"

"It — it must be a malfunction," Rackham said, his finger still firmly on the red activation switch.

"Then get out of there. Get out before the delta-V gets too high. We can still pick you up if you get out now."

"I can't get out," said Rackham. "The — the way to the EVA airlock is blocked."

"Then get into the *Soyuz* and cast off. God's sake, man, you're accelerating down toward the atmosphere."

"I — I don't know how to fly a *Soyuz.*"

"We'll get Kaliningrad to talk you through the separation sequence."

"No—no, that won't work."

"Sure it will. We can bring the *Soyuz* descent capsule into our cargo bay, if need be—but hurry, man, hurry!"

"Goodbye, Charlie."

"What do you mean, 'Goodbye'? Jesus Christ, Paul—"

Rackham's brow was slick with sweat. "Goodbye."

The temperature continued to rise. Rackham reached down and undogged his helmet, the abrupt increase in air pressure hurting his ears. He lifted the great fishbowl off his head, letting it fly across the cabin. He then took off the Snoopy-eared headset array. It undulated up and away, a fabric bat in the shaft of earthlight, ending up pinned by acceleration to the ceiling.

Paint started peeling off the walls, and the plastic piping had a soft, unfocused look to it. The air was so hot it hurt to breathe. Yuri's body was heating up, too. The smell from that direction was overpowering.

Rackham was close to one of the circular windows. Earth had swollen hugely beneath him. He couldn't make out the geography for all the clouds—was that China or Africa, America or Russia below? It was all a blur. And all the same.

An orange glow began licking at the port as paint on the station's hull burned up in the mesosphere. The water in the reticulum of tubes running over his body soon began to boil.

Flames were everywhere now. Atmospheric turbulence was tearing the station apart. The winglike solar panels flapped away, crisping into nothingness. Rackham felt his own flesh blistering.

The roar from outside the station was like a billion screams. Screams of the starving. Screams of the poor. Screams of the shackled. Through the port, he saw the Kristall module sheer clean off the docking adapter and go tumbling away.

Look below, the voice had said. *Look below.*

And he had.

Into space, at any price.

Into space—above it all.

The station disintegrated around him, metal shimmering and tearing away. Soon nothing was left except the flames. And they never stopped.

FEATURE INTERVIEW

Robert J Sawyer

This is the second time we've featured a story by Rob, the first being the urban fantasy 'Fallen Angel' in Issue 7, Summer 2015. This time we have psychological horror from Canada's Dean of SF. 'Above It All' was first published in 1996 in Dante's Disciples (edited by Peter Crowther and Edward E Kramer, White Wolf). Nearly thirty years later, it reads like historical fiction, but many of the protagonist's concerns are as pressing today as they were then. And yet some have been mitigated by science and evolving social consciousness. That alone gives us hope that the next few decades may solve the rest. And hope is something we desperately need in the face of the existential horror metaphorized so well in this fine tale.

Pulp Literature: *'Above It All' was written in 1995 and set in 2006. Of the many disasters over which the protagonist despairs, are there any that you see as improved? If you were to write this story today, would Colonel Rackham have reason to hope?*

Robert J Sawyer: I wish I could say yes, given that I'm known as an optimistic writer, but I'm afraid the world is in even worse shape than when I wrote 'Above It All' in 1995. Vladimir Putin has invaded Ukraine, and the notion of *Mir*—the Russian word for peace—just isn't relevant today. The idea of American and Russian cooperation in space or anywhere else seems ever more implausible.

And with Putin blocking grain shipments to needy people, the dichotomy between billions spent on space while humans are starving is more poignant than ever.

Don't get me wrong: I'm all in favour of space exploration, and I understand well the many benefits it has brought us. And I'd much rather see the public sector setting the agenda in space rather than the private-sector billionaires who are driving it now for capitalist reasons. But the world took a very dark turn in the last half decade, with the threat of nuclear holocaust returning, the rise of authoritarian leaders worldwide, a sharp shift to the right in many countries, and the complete denialism and failure to act related to climate change.

PL: *What futures are you afraid to imagine? Are there any stories you dare not tell?*

RJS: Not at all. If a science-fiction writer is afraid to tackle issues, they should give up the profession. Science fiction has a long and noble history of cautionary tales. Sadly, though, we who write the stuff are modern-day Cassandras: we've seen the potential downsides of our current trends, and we've been freely warning about them for many decades. But the public and, more importantly, the people in power just don't listen, whether it's our warnings over climate change, nuclear war, or the existential threat we're facing right now: the rise of artificial intelligence. Escapist science fiction doesn't interest me at all; I want to challenge my readers—and challenge myself.

PL: *You must have done extensive research for your excellent book* The Oppenheimer Alternative. *Given that J Robert Oppenheimer is the main character, what did you think of Christopher Nolan's movie* Oppenheimer?

RJS: It's a good film; I recommend it. But Cillian Murphy's brooding portrayal of Oppenheimer is awfully one-note. The real Oppie was much more complex—and much more charming! Still, Robert Downey Jr should get an Oscar for his subtle, perfectly controlled portrayal of Atomic Energy Commission chair Lewis Strauss. Matt Damon surprised me at how good he was as General Leslie R Groves. And Benny Safdie is pitch-perfect as Edward Teller.

But Nolan gives short shrift to almost all the other scientists—the larger-than-life but real characters I had so much fun portraying in my novel *The Oppenheimer Alternative*. And, if I may be so bold, for those real-life scenes that appear in both Nolan's movie and my novel, my portrayals are more historically accurate. I refused to change any of the things Oppenheimer actually said or did. Nolan had no compunction about that, and not one of his changes was an improvement over reality, in my view.

PL: *Do you have a well of inspiration to which you return?*

RJS: Yes: non-fiction reading, especially in science and ethics, and particularly the most recent works. When I teach science-fiction writing, I always ask my students what they're reading right now. It's astonishing that some aren't reading anything while others read nothing but science fiction—you need to read widely in literature if you're going to be a good writer, and most read no non-fiction at all. That leads into the second thing I tell my students: the old saying 'write what you know' is nonsense; one should write what they can find out about. And I love, love, love learning new things, and those things are what spark ideas for my fiction.

PL: *I understand from your blog that you are now on TikTok. Many writers we know struggle with finding a balance between creating writerly content for social media and doing the work of writing itself. How do you juggle these competing, but now entwined, worlds?*

RJS: Actually, I'm slowing down on social media. I really think the days in which social media made a significant impact for most authors have come and gone. It's simply too big an ask to expect people to stop scrolling on Facebook, or TikTok, or Twitter, and buy your book online, let alone go into a brick-and-mortar bookstore.

I had dinner with fellow best-novel Hugo Award winner Robert Charles Wilson recently, and we were both saying we just want to *write*, not hustle. At this stage in our careers, both Bob and I have found whatever audiences we're going to have, and we've been fortunate that they're big enough that we've had decades of making our livings off writing science fiction. But every minute spent on social media is one not spent writing, which is my first priority, or reading, which is my second. I have no desire to be a YouTube personality or a TikTok influencer. I just want to practise my art and enjoy the best work by other writers who also think of their work as art rather than commerce.

PL: *Thank you for making the time to speak with us. Before we go, tell us, what are you working on now?*

RJS: Going back to your question earlier, I'm tackling head-on what I suspect is a likely outcome of the current rise of artificial intelligence, namely dealing with a world in which humanity no longer has the reins of power. This novel, my twenty-fifth, will be called *Domestic Us*, and I suspect it'll shake up a lot of people — which is precisely what good science fiction is supposed to do.

SELECT BIBLIOGRAPHY

Golden Fleece (Aurora winner)
End of an Era (Seiun winner)
The Terminal Experiment (Nebula winner)
Starplex (Hugo and Nebula finalist)
Frameshift (Hugo finalist; Seiun winner)
Illegal Alien (Seiun winner)
Factoring Humanity (Hugo finalist)
FlashForward (Aurora winner)
Calculating God
Mindscan (Campbell Memorial Award winner)
Rollback (Hugo finalist)
Triggers
Red Planet Blues
Quantum Night (Aurora winner)
The Oppenheimer Alternative
The Downloaded
Domestic Us (forthcoming)
The Quintaglio Ascension trilogy
    Far-Seer
    Fossil Hunter
    Foreigner
The Neanderthal Parallax trilogy
    Hominids (Hugo winner)

    Humans (Hugo finalist)
    Hybrids
The WWW trilogy
    Wake (Hugo finalist, Aurora winner)
    Watch (Aurora winner)
    Wonder (Aurora winner)

STELLA RYMAN TAKES THE WHEEL

Mel Anastasiou

Mel Anastasiou writes the Fairmount Manor Mysteries, the Hertfordshire Pub Mysteries, and the Monument Studios Mysteries. Winner of a Literary Titan Gold award and longlisted for the Leacock Medal, Mel is also the author of two illustrated thirty-day workbooks on story structure: the steampunk-themed The Writer's Boon Companion and The Writer's Friend and Confidante. For news on published and upcoming new works, visit her website, melanastasiou.wordpress.com.

FAIRMOUNT MANOR

Stella Ryman Takes the Wheel

At Fairmount Manor, the saying goes, "Many leave for hospital, but few return." Now, in her city-wide search for Thelma Hu, Mrs Stella Ryman absconds with care worker Riley's Saab and heads downtown.

Stella leaned forward over the shabby leather-covered steering wheel of the somewhat stolen Saab she was driving northward through the city on her search for Thelma Hu. Ahead, a red light turned green above the northbound lane, sending a few lucky lunchtime drivers through the junction that should, in the fullness of time, lead her to the first of three bridges, and then downtown. It had been several years — and one institutionalization into Fairmount Care Home's driverless culture — since she had last travelled this road. It was no wonder she felt shaky; she was an elderly, rusty driver who'd eaten no lunch. However, even an escaped care home resident was no worse than this fool on her left, who was tailgating a purple van while signalling right. Such a move would, if she read his intentions correctly, take him directly into the Saab's driver-side door.

She frowned out of her window and waved the driver away. He responded by steering closer to her. She waved again, with the more imperious wave she had used in her days as an elementary-school teacher and librarian, when the end of recess found a few students still swinging from the monkey bars, oblivious to the movements of others and the passage of time.

Ahead, the light turned red again. The driver on her left buzzed down his passenger-side window. Stella opened hers.

The driver grinned at her. "Are you going to let me in, darling?"

Darling. Some things in the great world she'd thought she'd left forever didn't change. Some she missed, like hamburgers and garlic soup, but she did not miss fellows like this one, who snapped endearments at you like elastic bands off a ruler.

She said, "You will observe that our two lanes are moving at about the same rate of speed. I can't see why I should let you into this lane. Unless of course you're turning right up ahead. Are you?"

"No."

"Then you're exactly where you should be." She rolled up her window. The light turned green, and she and her neighbour moved ahead perhaps a dozen car lengths. He gestured at her to roll down her window again, and she did so.

He said, "I think I will turn right after all. Let me in now?"

She shot him an even look. "I tell you what: let's switch places."

"What, in line?"

"No," Stella said. "I'll get out and drive your car, and you can drive mine. Then you'll be in my lane. What do you think?"

The driver rolled up his window.

Stella drove the old Saab over the first bridge with the irritating driver just behind her left bumper. It was the perfect spot for him, out of her sight and hearing. Four cars ahead of her, the next stoplight turned red again, leaving her perfectly placed for the next green light. It was warm in the Saab, and Stella hung her elbow out the open driver's window in the manner of James Dean.

The obnoxious driver pulled up beside her. Clearly he'd had time to think up some new jibe, for he rolled down his window again.

"Are you all right in there?"

"Yes, thanks," Stella said. "One more green light and I think we're good to go over the second bridge."

"I only ask because your car seems very much past its prime."

"It's doing very well, actually."

"I only ask because it's so *very* old."

Stella blinked.

"It's just that I worry that you're going to break down in traffic. Because, you know, of *very old age*. For a *car*, I mean to say."

Stella tightened her hands on the Saab's distressed leather covered steering wheel. This fellow was a bit too accurate with his barbs.

She said, "Thanks for your worry. Really, I'm fine."

He said, "A car as old as that ought to be called by her first name. Have you named it?"

"I suppose I ought to name it," Stella said peaceably.

"Here's a good name: the *Old Grey Mare*," the other driver said.

When on earth was the light going to change? Stella squinted at the road ahead where cars still raced across the east-west route. But was that the walk sign winking orange? Hope rose in her heart. She felt like Daedalus, poised on the ledge, preparing to fly.

"This Saab is a *he*," Stella said. "His name—"

"How about *Oldstermobile*?"

"His name ..." Stella ransacked her brain for a name of glory. "This Saab's name is Icarus."

"Icarus?" The driver raised his eyebrows. "I saw that cartoon. Didn't he drop dead out of the sky? What a loser."

The light changed. Traffic moved, and the Saab pulled a little ahead of the rude fellow before he passed her again. She called out, "Icarus is a story of success, actually, not failure. He flew, didn't he?"

She would have added, *And every story ends in death eventually, just like every success,* but by the time she thought of saying this to him, he was darting in and out of the lanes ahead of her, rather like Icarus himself, if Icarus had been a snappy, discourteous middle-aged man.

She powered through the green light and drove along the causeway toward the first of the final two bridges that lay between her and the downtown hospital, where she intended to seek out Thelma Hu and take her home.

Traffic on the feeder road for the next bridge was no speedier than the first, and Stella and Riley's Saab moved ahead in stops and starts. Warm air, heavily scented with vehicular odours, was augmented by the midday sun's warmth through the window. Nonetheless, Stella felt grateful for Icarus's comfortable leather seats, and for the fact that her driver's licence had not yet expired. She had the right to drive, then, although not the card that proved her right. She had no idea where she'd left her licence. Maybe in the rubbish bin, where she'd tossed away all the other paperwork of her lifetime, a few months back when she sold everything to live at Fairmount Manor. But, if she understood the Internet correctly, her right to drive was somewhere out there.

She roared the engine, jumped forward a metre or so, and remembered that the Saab was an automatic and ought not to roar. She remembered the time, thirty years past, when she'd been rear-ended on this same bridge by a drunk who'd stopped, apologized, and then driven off into a lamppost. She had climbed out of her smacked Fiat and awaited help with her back to the bridge rails, while the rush of traffic tugged at her skirts. Which all went to prove that there had always been worse drivers than Stella out on the road.

Her stomach growled. Breakfast was a distant memory of brown toast and packet marmalade shared with Thelma and the Greek Chorus back at Fairmount. Now her appetite was out in the world and demanding real-world sustenance. She hadn't been this hungry since the autumn of 1976, when she'd done the eggs-only diet. She could almost smell the corned beef Kaiser bun with which she'd broken that diet once and for all.

Traffic stopped, and she looked out the windshield at a low-flying seagull with a bit of food in its beak. She smelled corned beef again and remembered that in the midst of all the red-hooded and Riley-flavoured kerfuffle back at the hospital, Sharon and Bethie had brought her a gift from the café. They had handed her a waxed paper bag just before the police officer had led that feckless, beer-soaked, occasionally well-meaning care worker Riley away for his DUI testing. She risked a glance to her right and, sure enough, there was the brown bag in the passenger seat at her side. The oily spots on the paper promised stains on the upholstery. Happily, they heralded as well an exuberant, fatty feed of the sort not to be found on Fairmount Manor luncheon plates.

Leaving her left hand ready on the steering wheel, she reached inside the bag, pulled out a toasted baguette, and glimpsed a red flash of corned beef within. At that thrilling moment, somebody behind Stella honked. She saw that the cars ahead of her were merging left. She set the baguette down and fumbled with her left turn signal. In the distance a police siren keened, and she checked the Saab's speedometer, but Icarus was travelling, like everybody else on the bridge, at a prim 32 kilometres an hour. A moment later she saw the reason for the slowdown: a police check at the end of an HOV lane. The midday sun shone down upon the black brim of the police officer's cap so that it glistened like the patent-leather pumps she had given her daughter Junie for her eighth birthday, many decades ago.

And then, in its happily unaccountable way, traffic sped up and cars lapped and were in turn lapped, all of them moving together onto the bridge leading north, with Icarus the Saab pulled along like a bead on a string. Stella made a conscious effort to lower her shoulders and breathe slowly. She eased her grip on the steering wheel and pressed her toe harder on the gas pedal. Icarus whipped past the checkpoint and onto the bridge on-ramp.

At the far end of the second bridge, Stella steered Icarus the Saab down the off-ramp in a glory of competence at the wheel. The nearly shadowless noontide darkened as she descended, and she noted as well that her bones felt rain coming, and coming on fast—as fast as the cars, speeding to either side of her now that they were off the bridge. Stella felt pure driver's delight at the ease with which she and Icarus kept pace with those around her. Even better, her sleuth's mind deduced a swift path northward to Thelma Hu, who waited for Stella without knowing that she was waiting for Stella. Thelma, who would be cursing the delay in her rescue and return to Fairmount Manor.

Stella changed lanes and passed a bus.

"Well done, Icarus," she murmured.

It made her feel a little giddy, talking aloud to a car without any worry that a care worker with rubber-soled shoes might slink up behind her, as so often happened in the serpentine corridors of Fairmount Manor. If care workers could hear her talking to Icarus now, they would think her gaga. Even Reliza, the kindest of them, or Cheryl of the Giaconda smile, would think she was losing her mind, chatting with a car.

"But I'm not losing my mind," Stella told Icarus the Saab. "I always used to talk to my cars—to my Chryslers, my Toyotas, my Hondas—and I would point out sights of interest. Or sing to them. Chryslers like Crosby, did you know? And Toyotas and Hondas enjoy Doris Day and Dinah Shore. What about Saabs? Do you like a little travelling music?" She patted at the radio knob, which came on with the local news, and patted it off again. Icarus's steering wheel slipped under her hand, and she narrowly missed winging the car next to her. She accepted what she considered a well-deserved bird from its driver.

"Sorry," she told its taillights.

On her right, three buses passed, big and noisy as aircraft on runways. And then the speed feast ended and the first of a busy series of traffic lights on the northbound avenue turned red.

"I'll sing to you while we wait for the light to change," she told Icarus. She sang 'Moon River' because, like everybody, she knew the words, and because it was a song about people who were stuck in their lane in the traffic of life. On the other side of the dashboard, beneath its battered hood, the Saab contributed a rattling percussion. It sounded as if something might be wrong with the motor, but not too wrong, because when the light changed, she and Icarus moved forward ten car lengths while 'Moon River' ran wide and the Saab hummed and flammed along. Another police siren sounded nearby, and it fit the descant pretty well. The sky opened over the city and added its own rhythms as rain drummed down on the windshield.

Signs and traffic lights merged into smears of colour against the grey city sky and street.

"Where do you keep your wipers?" Stella asked Icarus. She flipped a switch, inadvertently turned the emergency blinker on and off, beeped the horn, and found the wiper lever, all in a crazy five seconds. "Life with you is never dull," she said.

Icarus waved its windshield wipers at her like a fevered warning signal. *Stop, stop, stop.* Meanwhile, the traffic light showed green.

She was almost through the intersection when she observed that the cars to the front, back, and right of her were all police vehicles. Her neck stiffened. She wished to see whether any of the police officers in their squad cars and vans were looking her way, but the rain poured down harder and there was no way to tell. Her heart pounded, and her vision dimmed. She followed the blurry vehicle ahead of her and went through the light at the end of the yellow. The police cars travelled with her, and she and Icarus were boxed in. Lights flashed red from nearby police cars, and she was certain she'd be pulled over. But the uniformed drivers were only indicating a change of lane and a right turn. No siren sounded. In her relief, she wondered whether she should turn right with them. She liked a right turn.

She was shaking with more than hunger now, and it was all she could do to keep her eyes on the police car bumper and her hands on the wheel. Once all the police cars had turned east, she decided that she must pull over. It was parallel parking along this section of shops, nail bars, and sushi cafés, but she spotted two empty spaces together and nosed toward the curb. She set the parking brake and leaned her head against the steering wheel. Tears slipped down her cheeks.

The rain stopped. Sun poured into the Saab through the windshield.

Footsteps approached the passenger-side window, and the sound of rapping on glass brought Stella out of her funk. She jerked her head up from the wheel and peered at the rain-streaked window to see who might be anxious enough to demand her attention on such a busy street. Did somebody want a ride? She fervently hoped not.

Who would tap on a stranger's window, anyway? If only it was not a police officer. The tapping grew louder. But not loud enough for the law.

Stella felt dog-tired and about a million years old. She longed to close her eyes and let the tapper give up and move off, but she had learned early in her life that the true test of character was behaving agreeably toward others when all you really wanted was to get a cup of tea and pull the afternoon in around you. So she wiped her face with the collar of her shirt, rolled down the rain-smeared passenger window, and said hello to the figure outside on the sidewalk.

Two figures, rather: a man and a woman. The man bent down to look across at Stella. Behind him, the young woman's wet hair fell into her eyes, and she pushed it back. She wore a big black raincoat that didn't disguise her very advanced pregnancy. Was the woman at her full nine months? One couldn't inquire, of course. Stella recalled that she had recently driven away from a hospital. She tried to remember where it was. She supposed she could find it again, if this young woman needed her to transport her there.

Stella asked, "Do you need help?"

The man said, "I was going to ask you the same question. Are you all right? You looked like you were … upset."

"Crying," the woman added. "My husband and I wondered, are you hurt?"

"I wasn't really crying," Stella said. Her answer sounded untrue to her own ears, and furthermore her cheeks were wet. "I must just be very tired indeed. Thanks for your concern."

She expected the young couple would move away from the car, but they didn't.

"I don't want to intrude," the man said. "It's just you're parked about a foot and a half from the curb."

"It doesn't seem safe," the woman added.

"And you're in danger of stepping directly into traffic."

"It's scary parking in this kind of traffic," the young woman said. "I park too far out all the time, too."

Stella looked at the traffic outside the driver's window. The cars whiskered by her side mirror. She blinked, and her vision went blurry as it so often did under stress. A bus rattled the Saab as it passed, a hand's width away, and she heard the hiss of big tires on wet blacktop. Stella peered into her rear-view at the stream of traffic.

She said, "You're thoughtful. And correct. It doesn't seem safe. I'll just pull back into the empty space behind, I think, and narrow the gap …"

She put the Saab into reverse.

The young man and his wife uttered a simultaneous shout of warning. "Stop! The space isn't empty."

Stella looked over her shoulder and saw they were right. She felt herself colour. "Oh dear, I'll just ..."

She opened the driver's door to climb outside, and the two shouted again. Traffic whizzed by. It could have taken the Saab's door off.

The young man said, "You could have killed yourself stepping into traffic. Wait a minute." He walked around the front of the car and stood until the traffic flow stopped. He helped Stella out of the car and led her around the Saab and onto the sidewalk to his wife. "Would you like me to park your car for you?"

Stella had experienced the effects of morphine when she long ago gave birth to Junie, and the surge of cool relief at the young man's offer felt much the same. "That would be kind, thank you."

He returned to the Saab and sat behind the wheel.

The young woman took hold of Stella's arm in a comforting manner while her husband manoeuvred the Saab with swift jagged reversals closer to the curb. Once the car was pulled up tight and straight, he waited while a bus pulled into a stop a little further along the street, and then took advantage of a break in the traffic to exit the car. He came round the back, Stella's keys in hand.

The young woman said, "I don't think she's well at all. Maybe we could call someone."

Stella said, "No, thank you."

"Okay." The pregnant young woman and her husband exchanged a glance.

Stella said cautiously, "I have an idea that I'm not myself because I'm hungry."

"Let's get you something," the husband suggested. "Do you like sushi, dear?"

So soon after being *darlinged* by the lane-changing elder-baiting fellow, Stella noted with surprise that just now the word *dear* didn't sting. Perhaps the explanation was that, at this moment, beside the great buzzing insect that was city traffic, these two strangers were a little bit dear to her, too. In a *we-are-the-world, hands-across-the-generations* sense. This thought ought to have cheered Stella, but she felt too weak to be happy. And her fatigue made her too fuzzy to be certain she was not asking too much of this kind couple of strangers.

"Goodness, I couldn't possibly take advantage, but thank you."

"You must eat something, though."

The husband nodded at the Saab. "What about the lunch bag on the passenger seat?" He leaned into the car, partially unwrapped the baguette in its paper bag without touching the food, picked it up, and sniffed it. "This smells fine. Corned beef?"

"I thought it might be corned beef," Stella said cautiously.

"You'd better take it, hadn't you?"

"Heavens." Stella took the sandwich in its wrapping in her two hands. "It's enormous. Would you like some?" She held it out.

"No thanks." He looked at his wife. "What about some coffee?"

His wife nodded. "Good idea." She darted off, graceful for a pregnant woman. Stella wondered if she'd taken dance lessons when young. She was going to ask, but instead took a bite of the sandwich. She chewed and swallowed.

The young man asked, "How's that?"

"Very good indeed. And it's going straight to every cell in my body," she said.

"Coffee will do you good, too. Here. Sit on your passenger seat with your feet on the sidewalk."

Stella let him help her sit inside on the bucket seat with her feet resting on the sidewalk. She worked on her sandwich while the young man watched, dangling Stella's car keys from one hand. The young woman returned with two small paper cups that smelled of dark-roast beans. She gave one cup to her husband and set the other on the sidewalk within Stella's reach.

"Where's yours?" Stella asked.

The woman laughed. "I haven't been able to bear coffee for the last eight and a half months."

"For me it was eggs," Stella said. "It was very difficult, because I like omelettes, but then after my daughter was born, I liked eggs perfectly well again. If you've gone eight and a half months without coffee, then have you only two more weeks until the baby comes?"

"You're right on the mark," the woman said.

The husband said, "Can't wait for the birth day."

Stella wanted to ask what they meant to name the baby, but she had observed that over the last couple of decades many young parents appeared to dislike the question. She conjectured that they preferred to make the infant's acquaintance before settling on a name. Instead, Stella kept her curiosity to herself. She chewed some more of the superb corned beef baguette and sipped at the coffee.

Shoppers passed along the sidewalk, ran for the bus, and took away cups of hot drinks from the coffee shop. Stella ate and drank, at first like a child, but she sat up straighter and grew a little taller with each mouthful. The rain had thrashed about and confused her, and hunger had obfuscated her goal. Now she bent her thoughts again to finding and rescuing Thelma.

She said, "This was just what I needed. Thank you for your kindness, and for the coffee too."

She nodded at the car keys.

The two young people exchanged another look.

"Where do you live?" The husband asked. "Do you trust us to drive you there?"

Stella imagined pulling up to Fairmount Manor in Riley's car, without Riley, and facing the unwelcome explanations that would ensue. Worse, any further escapes from Fairmount would necessitate what Stella had come to think of as the long game. She didn't have time for the long game. Thelma was alone, in hospital, and in some ways nearly as vulnerable as this woman's baby would be when it was born.

"Thanks, but I think I'll be all right," she said. She folded the last quarter of her baguette back into the bag and reached up for the Saab's keys.

The young husband exchanged another look with his wife. He glanced down at the keys in his hand. "I don't know," he said.

"We don't want you to be hurt," his wife said.

"Why would I be hurt?" Stella asked. She tried to not to show that she was irked at the suggestion. The overcautious signs around Fairmount were bad enough, with their *residents must not climb the stairs, residents cannot bathe alone,* without hearing the same kind of doubts here on the city street from people who didn't even know she'd had herself committed to a care home.

A man in a cap walked out of the coffee shop with a paper cup in each hand. He chuckled as he approached the tableau the three of them made, and looked on as Stella reached out to take the keys from the young husband's hand.

The man in the cap said to Stella in jolly tones, "If you want my opinion, lady, you'll do the world a favour and hand in your licence. Over eighty, you shouldn't drive."

Stella said, "You might discover you feel differently when you're eighty yourself."

"I think when I turn eighty I'll trade my car in for a chainsaw," he answered. "That way, if I lose my mind in a senior moment, I'll only kill myself and not a bunch of people at a bus stop." He nodded at a bus that pulled up a few yards further along the road to downtown.

"Yeah, okay," the wife said. "You've made your point."

Her husband added, "Thanks for your concern, guy." He shot Stella a glance that might have been sympathy, or possibly a warning to keep still.

"Just a word to the old and wise …" The man tapped his nose with one of his cups of coffee. His gesture knocked the lid off the cup and spilled coffee down his shirt. He cursed and walked off.

Stella looked up at the two young people. "I don't drive much, I promise you, but I absolutely must drive downtown. I have to fetch a friend who's alone and afraid in hospital."

"Have you phoned to make sure your friend is still there?"

"I have a phone at home but not with me. It's rather an old model. But I'm almost sure she's there."

"What's her name?" The young woman reached into her raincoat pocket and brought out her phone.

"Thelma Hu."

"There's only one hospital downtown, right?"

The young woman talked into the phone and then replaced it in her pocket. She said to Stella, "They have workmen everywhere at the hospital this week, and with all the work on their networks, boxes, and cables, their computers are down again. You can phone back in an hour … How's our time, sweetie?"

"We have about ten minutes spare."

"That won't get us downtown to her friend in the hospital and back."

Stella said, "I'm fine to drive now."

"Well, see, that guy was a jerk, but he was a jerk with a valid point," the man said.

"I do still have my driving licence." This was starting to feel like one of those school meetings where a kindly administrator was leading the discussion toward extreme cuts to her library budget. Stella talked cheerfully on, as she had always done when the rumour was that all spare funds would go to team uniforms and not to books. "I don't have my licence with me, but it will still be on record."

"Well, sure. But we're just worried that you'll get into another fugue state."

Fugue state. The foggy condition was disconcerting and embarrassing, but Stella decided that overall she liked the appellation *fugue.* It was certainly better than *senior moment. Fugue state* sounded like something Mozart might have experienced if he'd lived to be an elderly genius. Stella pictured Mozart at eighty, or even ninety, his white hair tied back, driving a four-in-hand along a Paris boulevard.

She said, "I promise, no more fugue states."

"I don't think that's something you can promise, though."

"Good old Icarus will get me there."

"Icarus?"

"Because he can really fly. But I won't go too fast. You see, I'm very careful." Somewhere, she supposed Mozart was laughing at her and urging his team of matched horses to greater speeds.

"Didn't Icarus fall?" the young woman asked. "It's not a happy story."

"On the contrary." Stella smiled. "It was a very happy story, except for the bit at the end."

"The bit where the father watched his son fall to his death?" The wife touched her belly with the flat of her hand.

Stella deduced the young people's message. It was the same old warning. The imprecation many folks felt compelled to offer but she disliked to receive. *Be safe. Death can and must be avoided.* Their attitude was understandable and even sound. Still, she wished that she in turn could communicate to them what death looked like from her view, away out here toward the end of life. From here, you didn't fear death as a sort of kidnapping or blow. Death was more like a mysterious darkness kept at bay by the fiery torch of life, a flame that might or might not keep burning, and around which you gathered with those companions who saw it too: Theo and the Greek Chorus back at Fairmount, for example. The Rose Corridor women. And Thelma Hu, somewhere in this city, lying in a strange hospital bed, practically blind and entirely alone, with no friend to wake her at sunrise and sit with her at night.

But Stella couldn't say that. Or she wouldn't. Not with the exact opposite occasion coming up so soon for these two young people. She thought of this young woman's baby, and of her own Junie, tiny in her arms long ago. It occurred to her that she might never hold a newborn child again in her lifetime. She had noticed since arriving at Fairmount that endings happened without her noticing: the last newborn she'd held, the last milkshake she'd sucked through a straw, the final time she'd read her favourite book.

Stella said, "You know, I might just take the bus downtown."

Relief broadcast itself from both young people.

"That's a really good idea," said the mother of the unnamed future baby.

Her husband helped Stella up. He peered inside the Saab. "Is your handbag in here, or anything you need?"

Stella had no handbag. It was a point of pain with her. But she touched her right-hand trouser pocket, full of the cash Vaughn had given her. "I've got everything I need right here."

"Will I put the rest of your baguette into the trash or leave it in the car?"

Stella considered the question. It would be pleasant for Riley to find a half-eaten baguette on the passenger seat of his Saab, but hardly kind to the Saab itself.

"Into the trash, please."

The young man binned the baguette and closed and locked the Saab doors.

"Good luck," the young woman said. "Do you want me to telephone the hospital downtown to let somebody know you're coming?"

Stella observed the woman check her watch and said, "Let's not give them any advantage. I'll take them by surprise."

They laughed, and the husband said, "We've got to leave you right now if we're going to make our appointment. Here are your keys."

"Thanks." Stella tucked them in her right-hand pocket. "Thanks for all your help. And my good wishes for your new life with your lovely child."

"It's a girl," the woman said. "We asked."

"Oh, how wonderful," Stella said.

The couple waved, turned, and walked away. Before he'd gone ten steps, the husband turned back, and his wife looked up at him. He called out, "What's her name?"

"I'm Stella," she answered. "Stella Ryman."

"No, what's your daughter's name?"

Stella blinked. "Junie."

"June or Junie?"

"Junie." She smiled at them, remembering the sunlit inspiration that had sent her that particular name. A sunny day, much like today.

"Good name," he said.

"Junie," the woman said.

They waved again, and Stella watched them walk along the sidewalk. She would have watched them walk out of sight, but she spotted a bus at the light. Its sign read *Downtown.*

Once the young couple had left her alone on the sidewalk, Stella took a moment to stand casually beside the Saab and jingle the car keys in her pocket, as one did. She felt an unexpected sense of quiet confidence in her role as an escapee, acting insouciant beside a stream of passers-by. Most of them walked quickly past her and out of view along the sidewalk, north or south; several passed into the coffee shop. A few entered the sushi place to the left of the coffee shop, and one person entered and then exited the Dollars4More store to the coffee shop's right. She smiled to see on display the same Canadian-themed tea towels that students had from time to time given her for June thank-you gifts. Her own national icon tea towels had, of course, worn out over time and finished as cleaning rags, their bright patterns unrecognizable by the end. But here they were again, miraculously and delightfully unchanged except in price, and available for purchase if, like Stella, one had money in one's pocket. Stella could buy a lot of tea towels with the money Vaughn had given her. She smiled to think what flabbergasted expressions Annie and Enid, the Fairmount Manor cooks, would wear if they took delivery of crates of matching moose-emblazoned tea towels for their institutional kitchen.

But daydreaming about a glorious return to Fairmount wouldn't bring Thelma home. Stella needed to move her quest forward if she were to find her friend this afternoon. Car keys in hand, she watched another bus pass the parked Saab. Now that her two young rescuers had left her with the keys, it would be simple to pull out into traffic and drive downtown. The obfuscating rain showed no sign of returning anytime soon. She felt a twinge of self-reproach and swiftly banished it. After all, she had not promised them that she wouldn't drive. She hadn't stated outright that she would take the bus. All she had said was that she was thinking about it. And she was.

The bus for downtown stopped a few yards up the way from the store. Passengers stepped off and passengers stepped on. Stella hadn't ridden a bus in about twenty years, but the passengers made it look easy. The bus doors flapped and closed, front and rear. Nothing new there. The steps to the doors were lower than she remembered, and much closer to the curb. Back when she was a girl, well before she got her driver's licence, bus steps had been cliffs of high black rubber which, more often than not, let her out to leap a small blacktop chasm beside a leaf-clogged gutter.

The bus pulled away. Stella took the Saab keys out of her pocket and held them up. The sun shone nearly straight down on the keys, and they flashed like a warning light. A second bus whooshed past without stopping, and Stella put the keys back in her pocket.

She moved toward the bus stop and joined a queue of four people. She had no idea how much fares were now—like the moose and beaver tea towels, they must have climbed in price—but she remembered bus drivers very well: they did not suffer gladly making change from large denominations, and they did not hesitate to order people off the bus. She dug in her pocket and pulled out a hundred-dollar bill. When she tried again, she saw it was a fifty. Stella registered the curious glance of a young fellow ahead of her, tucked her fifty-dollar bill away, and stepped back from the queue. The young fellow got on the bus, and she returned his stare through the window as it pulled away.

The young man's interest in her cash was a clear harbinger of fiscal complications. She must get change for at least one of her large bills. She turned on her heel and walked into the Dollars4More store.

The first observation Stella made at the Dollars4More store was that there was not much priced at a dollar except for candies and sparkly pencils. A lucky thing, too, because she needed to break a large bill into change for the bus. She couldn't pay for a sparkly pencil or a bag of candies with a hundred-dollar bill. Nor could she carry ninety pencils around with her. She could bin them when she left the shop, but that seemed a mean trick to play upon sparkly pencils, a small evil act without consequence, ethically repugnant to her. She needed to buy something small, portable, and more expensive. Further, it was a moral imperative that she buy something she desired, or else why had she accepted Vaughn's cash gift? She studied the goods set out upon shelves and display tables around the store and thought that it was rather like Woolworth's long ago, with its open-top cases of lipstick, key chains, and fragile plastic toys.

In the here and now, the crookedly stacked cat-shaped candles seemed as unlikely to sell today as forty years ago. She was struck by the sight of dozens of crazy rainbow wigs on stands skirting the walls, for she remembered a time when wigs were serious business and one thought hard about which style to purchase for, say, a trip overseas, when one's standing weekly hair appointment must be missed.

The fellow behind the cash desk gazed at her across displays of impulse-buy chocolate and taco chips. He gave her a charming smile, but no matter how friendly his presence, he'd never have been hired at Woolworths, not even in the seventies, with his hair so long and tied up in a topknot.

He asked, "Looking for anything in particular, or something at large?"

Stella answered, "Not really. I guess I'll know what I want when I see it."

"You're my kind of customer. Likely to buy, unlikely to shoplift. Have at it."

He took out a paperback book and bent over it. It was a classic English-language edition of Voltaire's *Candide, ou l'Optimisme.*

"Candide?" Stella said. "I'm impressed."

The cashier looked sheepish. "Well, to be fair, I finished a werewolf YA this morning."

"Maybe werewolf YAs will turn out to be the great classics in the twenty-third century," Stella said.

The cashier laughed. "If I live that long, I guess I'll be all studied up."

Stella strolled off to find something among the Dollars4More store wares that she could buy to make change for the bus. As she moved among the shelves and tables, she noticed the convex mirrors at various corners and angles of the merchandise space. And the cashier glanced up from his book every ten seconds or so. As an amateur detective, she considered this an efficient method for the cashier to enjoy his book while in sole charge of a business where much of the stock was shiny and of a size to fit up one's sleeve. She wandered among the glittering merchandise, while in the clerk's book — and Stella's memory — Candide pursued his Cunégonde across the shark-infested seas. Stella too was in pursuit of a woman, and her friend and care-home co-conspirator Thelma Hu was, in Stella's opinion, far more deserving of rescue than Voltaire's feckless and inconstant heroine. Cunégonde would have liked this store, though. Especially when she perceived that some of the gimcrack necklaces were actually lavalieres. And only eight dollars.

Notwithstanding this excellent price and the attractive symmetry of buying a lavaliere from a clerk reading Voltaire, Stella had long ago rejected the lampooned philosophy of *L'Optimisme,* and so she decided on principle not to buy eight-dollar necklaces. She searched the shelves for something less glittery but equally portable.

She found the best of all possible items in a shopping section that she had never thought to buy from again: the travel section. Here were foam neck pillows that she might have appreciated the last time she's flown to Voltaire's Paris, and here also hung travel handbags that looked quite a bit like leather — *genuine Naugahyde* was a joke that never aged in Stella's mind. One of the bags reminded her heartbreakingly of her old leather handbag with embossed sides that she'd brought back from a school vacation in Mexico and which, when opened, had always smelled of pack animal.

A rack of travel security accessories caught her eye and brought her back to the exigent present. The boxes were labelled *Krownkind Security Triple Pack.* She picked one off the shelf and peered at the contents through the translucent box top. This pack of three items might have been designed for her own personal use. However, it was priced far higher than the surrounding merchandise.

She patted her pocket where she carried the money Vaughn had given her back at Fairmount. Why not use her cash power and buy herself some security? In fact, why not have a little spree and buy two boxes? Stella was certain that she wasn't the only one who could use a Krownkind Security Triple Pack. She picked a second box off the rack and walked with one in each hand toward the register.

She was about to set her purchases on the counter for the topknotted young man with the book to ring up when the front door opened and a police officer entered. There was likely no reason a police officer should not enter this place of business. Equally, Stella had done nothing to invite even casual detainment for questioning except steal Riley's car. Nevertheless, Stella felt an almost primal need to pay and escape. With swift movements, she placed her selections in front of the cashier and fumbled with the folded bills in her pocket. A hundred came free, and two further hundreds fell out of her pocket onto the floor, out of the cashier's view.

Stella held onto the counter to keep her balance while she snatched one hundred-dollar bill from the floor, but the second one slid away and under a nearby display table. Footsteps approached behind her, and into Stella's limited view came the police officer's comfortable black shoes and trousered legs. With swift dispatch, the hand of the law reached down to pick up Stella's errant hundred-dollar bill. The police officer waited as Stella straightened up. She handed the hundred to her.

Stella thanked her and tucked two of the hundreds back into her pocket. She handed the third to the clerk to pay for her security packs. It did not escape Stella that all the while she was keeping an eye on the police officer, the police officer had her eye on Stella as well, or rather on Stella's lumpy, cash-filled pocket.

While she waited for the cashier to ring up the Krownkind Security Triple Pack, Stella avoided the officer's gaze by scanning the merchandise in the innocent manner of a frequent consumer of dollar-store merchandise. When her eye settled upon the travel section, she was rewarded with an idea so excellent that she wanted to kick herself for almost missing it.

"Please cancel the sale," she said. "I want to add to my purchase, if you don't mind."

The cashier set down his book.

"Sorry," she said. "I just thought of something I've been needing for a long time."

"Don't apologize. You're adding to the rich pageant of my day," the clerk said. "Furthermore, they pay me to just do that sort of thing."

He cancelled the sale, and Stella walked past the police officer back to the travel section. There she took down from its hook the travel handbag that looked so much like her own Mexican bag and returned with it to the desk. It was the most profligate purchase she had made in at least a year, but she still got change back from her hundred—certainly enough change to get her onto the bus. The cashier filled a plastic bag with the two security packs. Stella told him that she wanted to carry this excellent handbag right away, and he removed the wadded-up paper inside it and handed it to her with a flourish. She thanked him and dropped the change from her transaction into her new handbag, which was so empty she could almost hear an echo from the rattle of coins and rustle of small bills.

She glanced at the police officer and caught the woman still staring at Stella's bulging pockets.

The police officer addressed the clerk. "Is there a washroom I could use?"

The clerk pointed at a sign on the wall behind the cash desk: *No public washroom.*

"Do I look like the public?" the police officer asked.

The cashier nodded acceptance and indicated a door beyond the lavalieres section that read *Employees Only.* Stella decided that she would ask to use it after the police officer. But in the event, she didn't need to ask, because the police officer turned to Stella and said, "Ma'am, please come with me."

Stella gripped her purchases against the front of her fleece jacket and followed the police officer into the small, barely serviceable staff washroom. With her arms full and the public representative of the law standing so close, the lumps of money in her pockets felt enormous.

The police officer took the handbag and the two Krownkind Security Triple Packs in their plastic bag and set them carefully upon the back of the toilet.

She said, "It's about that money in your pocket."

Stella put her hand into her pocket and pulled out the wad of cash. It filled her two hands. Such was the quiet power of the officer's tone that it was all Stella could do not to hand the lot of it over.

"It's mine," Stella assured her. She couldn't help adding, "I haven't declared it on my income tax yet, as it will be for next year's return."

"I know it's your money." The officer grimaced. "I'm afraid this is a very common problem."

"Elderly ladies with money?"

"Always. My aunt was the same. She kept at least a thousand dollars, in cash, in her fridge freezer. And sometimes she kept it in an old men's jacket on her hat rack. And somebody came in the house, found it, and stole it."

"Oh, dear, how awful for her," Stella said. She thought, *What an idiot that aunt must be to keep money in places like that.*

"We get lots of complaints about cash stolen from pensioners. Sometimes we catch the thief."

"I would think that it would be difficult to prove somebody had stolen cash."

"Usually, the victims don't even know how much they had," the police officer said. "Which brings me to the point. I'm worried to see you walking around with all those hundreds bulging in your pocket. You're a real target for thieves."

Stella was about to say that in her experience most people were honest, but it seemed a foolish thing to say to a police officer; as well, she remembered the young man in the bus line-up who had eyed her high-denomination cash with such interest. She said, "What should I do?"

"Don't worry, I know better than to tell you to put it in the bank. There are only so many brick walls I'm willing to talk to. Let's see." The police officer took Stella's new handbag from her and looked inside it. "Not bad. Anti-cutting strap, so it's difficult to snatch. And a side pocket for most of your money. Too bad this one doesn't come with a wallet …"

Stella, almost giddy with triumph, produced one of the two Krownkind Security Triple Packs from its shopping bag. "What do you think of this?"

She was rewarded by a look of reassessment from the police officer. The officer opened the plastic box and pulled up the first of the three items. This was a wallet, the kind that stops thieves from reading and copying your cards electronically. Stella had no cards, of course, but she took back her new handbag and pulled out her change in small bills and coins. The police officer held the wallet open and Stella placed this money inside it.

The police officer looked from the remaining bundle of money to the slender neoprene wallet. "Well …"

Stella placed the wallet inside the handbag's interior zip pocket. "Look in the box again, officer."

The officer looked, blinked, and pulled out a long bit of folded nylon. It was beige, and it had a zipper.

"Goodness. That's a money belt. And wide enough to take all that cash, if you don't mind the inches around your middle. Right. Let's strap you up."

She folded the money and tucked it inside the belt, which expanded in unflattering directions but contained the mass of notes of large denomination.

"Will you please fit it round me?"

"Okay, lift that jacket up." The police officer negotiated the clipping of her belt around Stella's waist.

"Thank you." Stella tugged at it to make sure the clip would hold.

"Tuck it inside your underwear as well, don't you think?"

This rarely-referenced travel tip was not new to Stella after her many foreign adventures in the real life she'd left behind when she sold everything to move to Fairmount Manor. Back in her travelling days, and again now, she would rather her assets fell into her underwear than onto the ground.

"I'm tucked," Stella said.

"What's this third thing?" The police officer held up the articulated invention that had first attracted Stella's attention and then her imagination. Stella knew the item's purpose but she didn't want to explain it — or her excitement at having purchased two of them. The last subject she wanted to visit with this figure of legal authority was Fairmount Manor and its mores and red tape, nor how these purchases would help with her ongoing mission to put wrenches into the machineries of institution. So Stella shrugged and kept silent while the police officer packed the remaining travel items into the new handbag, which plumped it out nicely. She looped the handbag's cross-body strap over Stella's head and settled it onto her shoulder.

"Now, where are you off to?" the police officer asked.

Stella considered the question. She wondered whether she ought to tell this helpful and apparently under-occupied officer of the law that she was on a mission to help a blind friend in the hospital downtown. She had an idea that a ride in a police car might be a swift and direct flight to her goal, so much so that she was reminded of Icarus and his joyful, daring rise and fatal descent. If she were to fly too close to the law, she might find herself falling amid the scattered feathers of her goals and independent decisions to land not at Thelma's side in hospital but back down in Fairmount's corridors and the roiling sea of restricted movement and paucity of options. If so, as with Icarus, her trip would have been a success right up to its inevitable failure. And Thelma would still be alone in the hospital.

When Stella didn't reply to her query, the police officer frowned, and the atmosphere in the little washroom changed subtly. "Ma'am, are you going home?"

"Of course. Look, I'm so sorry to ask," Stella said, "but we're in the washroom, and I need to use it. Do you mind?"

The police officer's expression cleared. "Not at all. I'm going to buy that candy bar I came in for."

"*Bon appétit.*" Stella locked the washroom door and was happy to remain completely honest in her dealings with the law by using the facilities.

Then she waited. Like a spy, like the sleuth she was, she listened from behind the locked door. Distantly, she made out the sound of the policewoman answering her phone and then the clacking noise of a door opening and closing. Had another customer entered, or had the police officer left? She could detect no further sounds of conversation, nor any other clues to the situation in the store itself. The police officer had been kindness personified, and yet if Stella emerged too soon, the officer's helpful hand on her shoulder would undoubtedly reveal itself to be the implacable hand of the law.

Stella decided to give it another ten minutes and passed the time inspecting her new wallet and handbag. She was adjusting the cross-body strap buckle up a notch when a knock sounded at the door. "Hello?"

Stella held her breath.

The cashier spoke through the door. "Sorry, but I need to use the washroom."

"Of course." Stella washed her hands and exited. The police officer was nowhere in sight. Stella asked the cashier, "What do you do about the store when you're in there? Do you have to lock the front door?"

"I lock the register," he said, "and I, um, hurry."

"Sorry. And thanks for your help."

"Welcome." He disappeared inside.

Stella exited what she now considered to be a Panglossian ideal of a shop.

Out on the street, she adjusted her new handbag and experienced a peculiar desire to show off her purchase to Icarus the Saab parked neatly at the side of the road. She opened the car door and considered climbing in. But, without warning, her conscience struck her a stunning blow. She dropped the car keys into her new bag and remembered that the car was not hers. So she tucked the keys under the seat, pushed the lock home, and closed the passenger-side door. With one hand on Icarus's sun-warmed hood, caressing it as she might a dog or a child before letting it roam free, she scanned the sidewalk for the police officer without result. Passers-by walked swiftly north or south and didn't glance in her direction, apparently lost in thought or checking their phones. Somebody came out of the sushi bar with a plastic box, and somebody else went into the Dollars4More store. Stella decided that this area of town had nothing more to give her. Even Icarus the Saab couldn't help her now.

A bus heading downtown approached, and Stella moved into place in the short queue. She had just enough time before boarding to take a handful of change from her new wallet, confident that some combination of coins would get her where she was going.

She climbed up after the first three passengers and held out the coins to the driver.

He looked from the coins to her face. He pointed to the small notice posted at the front of the bus. Stella read the warning, apparently meant for thieves, that no money was kept on the bus.

"I need your card, please."

Stella wondered what card.

"Did you forget it?"

Soldier on, Stella. "I suppose I did."

The bus driver sighed. It was not an angry sigh, more a seen-it-all-before sigh. He closed the door behind her and pulled out into traffic. "Hold on, please."

She said, "I forgot the card's existence, if I ever knew it. I haven't actually ridden a bus for twenty years."

He asked, "Is it an emergency?"

"That's perceptive of you. Yes, I have a friend in the hospital, and she's blind, and ..."

"If it's an emergency, and you can't pay, then please take your seat."

Stella was gobsmacked. "But you could lose your job, transporting people for free."

Stella felt a tug at her sleeve. A grey-haired woman in the front seat of the bus nearest the driver gestured urgently at the seat beside her. "They do have to let you ride if it's an emergency, so don't worry about him."

The bus driver pulled over again, and a couple of people got on. One of them was a girl with a knit hat and a tattered backpack. "It's an emergency," she said in earnest tones. The bus driver waved her on board. Stella wasn't sure whether it was proper to hope the youngster was lying and there was no real emergency, or whether to hope she told the truth and so justify Stella's generalized faith in the younger generation.

She glanced at the friendly passenger beside her. The woman appeared to be at least as old as Stella and perhaps older. But, unlike Stella in her washed and worn fleece warm-up suit, this woman wore crisp trousers, a buttoned tunic not made of fleece, sensible shoes, and a silk scarf tied in the French manner and tucked into her tunic.

Stella asked, "Do you know, does this bus stop at the hospital downtown, or will I need to transfer?"

The woman smiled. "I took the bus to that particular stop every day of my working life. Yes, it does stop at the hospital. I hope you're not ill?"

"I've a friend alone in hospital," Stella said. "I'm hoping to find her there."

"Good for you," the woman said.

"Thanks. You look like you still have a vigorous life going," Stella said. "What's your secret? So many of us are in care."

"You're not, obviously."

Stella hesitated. "I've thought about it."

"Those thoughts come to everybody. But not everybody should listen to them. At least not too soon."

"What, then?"

"Philosophy, that's what. When I first retired from nursing, I said to myself, try not to get old, but take all the perks of age that are going."

"What a good motto."

"Well, it's just what I thought up—not much of a motto really. You've obviously got your own philosophy or you'd be in one of those care homes, wouldn't you?" She rose and touched a button on the upright pole by the driver's seat. "But sometimes a person can't care for themselves, and then I guess it's a care home or nothing. I hope your friend feels better." The woman moved toward the door. "I'd have thought it more likely she's in General than downtown, with all that's going on there."

"What do you mean?" Stella recalled with a start the pregnant woman's attempt to call the hospital downtown and the report of computers being down. "Is something wrong at the hospital?"

"Not at all. It's just progress, isn't it? I'm sure you watch the news …"

The bus driver opened the door, and the woman thanked him and stepped down.

Stella rode on. She puzzled at the retired nurse's mention of the hospital in the news but got nowhere. Outside the bus window, the storefronts flashed multicoloured reflections at her, and the May afternoon sunshine warmed her bones. The bus moved slowly on, making stop after stop, purring and rocking along the long road downtown so that Stella had to pinch the inside of her arm to keep from nodding off. If she slept past the hospital stop, Thelma might never know, but Stella would never forgive herself.

§

Don't miss the final act of Stella Ryman and the Search for Thelma Hu, *coming in Issue 41.*

Also by Mel Anastasiou

THE EXTRA: A MONUMENT STUDIOS MYSTERY

Vancouver schoolmarm Frankie Ray runs away to Silver Screen Hollywood to test her conviction that an actress who lacks glamour but has talent and an enterprising attitude can make it in the movies. But when a dissolute, womanizing matinee idol turns up dead on her sofa, Frankie's career hopes shatter. She'll need all her acting chops to sleuth out the murderer and clear her name.

STELLA RYMAN AND THE FAIRMOUNT MANOR MYSTERIES

On this particular sun-and-shade April morning at Fairmount Manor, Stella Ryman no more entertained the idea of becoming an amateur sleuth than she did of entering next spring's Boston Marathon. For not only was Stella eighty-two years old, but she had lately sold her home and a lifetime of gathered possessions and washed up at Fairmount Manor Care Home in such a state that she would have bet her remaining seven pairs of socks that she'd be dead in half a year.

THE LABOURS OF MRS STELLA RYMAN:
FURTHER FAIRMOUNT MANOR MYSTERIES

When the machineries of institution fail to protect Fairmount Manor, octogenarian amateur sleuth Mrs Stella Ryman rolls up her fleece jacket sleeves to protect Fairmount from a thief, investigate a gun-toting resident, set right a mishandled investigation of a man's death, pursue spectres and footpads walking at midnight, and discover Thelma Hu's long-lost fortune. No good deed goes unpunished, though, and Stella will face struggles, mysteries, and sacrifices that hit her where she lives.

PULPLITERATURE.COM

THE LADY M
Cat Girczyc

Cat Girczyc *works as a technical communications manager while pursuing creative writing at night. Her work appears in* On Spec, Tesseracts, Neo-Opsis, Polar Borealis, *and elsewhere. And in 2020 she won a Women in Film & TV #FromOurDarkSide award for her script* Lights, Camera, Paranormal Action. *She's a Writers Guild of Canada member and has sold 15 television episodes, including two episodes of the dark fantasy* The Collector *and the animated series* Cybersix. *'The Lady M' was a finalist in the 2022 Writers of the Future (WOTF) competition, Quarter 1.*

The Lady M

The first time that I can remember noticing men was in Old Québec. I was stealing eggs from that wonderful innovation, the chicken coop, and I met a man in a brown robe who felt he owned not just the chickens but all of the eggs as well. I'd since become civilized, or perhaps that was my protector Jack's influence. Jack was a good sugar daddy to me, but now I wanted kits.

Am I long-lived? Yes, but I do hibernate — for decades. When I'm human, the mirror shows me a tall, elegant woman with black hair and a broad white streak. I looked about thirty years old when I met Anton Bogdanovich Petrov in the antiquated Sylvia Hotel bar next to English Bay and my favourite hunting ground, Stanley Park.

He was as handsome a human as they come. A long, lean, muscular man with bright blue eyes and curly blond hair. He claimed to be related to Russian princes of the century before. Even I knew there had been no Russian princes alive to procreate at the time of his birth in the late twentieth century. So initially, I kept my distance.

"C'mon and have a drink with me, my mysterious beauty," he'd tease me in his accented English, night after night. I saw him regularly that summer. He sat by the window, next to my favourite table by the mirror that reflected English Bay. It had been a long time since I'd had a new friend, and I was wary of friends. *He* had a lot of friends, many of whom didn't look like friendly people. I pick my acquaintances carefully. Not like those over-trusting dog-family werewolves who always end up on the end of a peasant's pitchfork no matter how close they think they are to the family in question.

One summer dusk, when the rain threatened and I felt like watching a storm on the water, I went to the Sylvia earlier than usual. Only Anton and I were there. It seemed impolite to refuse his offer of a drink.

"What does a beautiful woman like you do here? Drinking alone always?" he asked.

"Oh, I read and await my friends," I replied.

"But you are always alone."

"Not tonight," I replied, smiling. The kit with the cream smile.

"What are you called?"

"Lady Mephitidae."

"Do you have a first name?"

"Maybe I'll tell you sometime if you become my friend."

So I, Lady Mephitidae the Skunk-girl, drank with Anton the Russian all night. He told me fantastical tales of his relatives at home, one of whom was a robber baron, now called an oligarch, who could get Anton anything he wanted and paid him for computing enterprises not entirely legal or moral.

Anton drank too much Stoli and told me he supported his mother, who lived with him. She was somewhat addicted to gambling and loved the casino in Richmond. He shook his head. She'd had a hard life, and what could one do? He seemed kind.

He had a girlfriend, too, he confessed—a model.

"Why aren't you with her tonight?"

"She loves shopping more than me," he said. "She's very beautiful. All of my friends are impressed with her."

I frowned, wondering why he was talking to me. Was he one of those men who cannot see a female alone without making a pass? Foolish him, then.

"Look, Lady, I'm not asking you to make love to a man who already has a girlfriend. Even I am not that bold." He smiled, and I knew he was lying.

That night, we had many vodkas, and I paid, as I do, with a platinum card that Jack, my mining-magnate friend, supplied. My old friend was one reason I hesitated with Anton. Jack had kept my secret so very long, and now, at 95, was failing. His children had long ago moved to Toronto and New York; he was a widower and alone. I remembered him from when he'd been a suave Cary Grant type in the fifties. We went to Miami Beach on lost weekends, stayed at ritzy hotels, walked the white-sand beach, and visited the Everglades. He kept my secret, and I never went near his wife or family. Our arrangement was perfect, or had been.

The morning after the night of many vodkas, my head hurt. I do not metabolize alcohol well. I hid in the bushes near the tennis courts most of the day, lying around in my comfy black-and-white fur coat, avoiding tourists and coyotes.

Two days later I looked in my closet. I wanted something new. Hermes scarf on, I hailed a taxi to Holt Renfrew. Anton was promising, and I was enticed. I wanted something flirty but gorgeous. I picked the ideal little black dress from Chanel.

There was an aura of consternation at the checkout. I was aware of a chill from my usually fawning personal shopper. She took me aside. My platinum card had been rejected. *Quelle horreur!* There was a note that I must call the company, which I did immediately. The credit card people were not happy. Someone had maxed out my card. Oh, and stolen my identity.

True, it was a flimsy identity, but I needed one in the modern world. Gone were the days when I could just open a bank account while Jack grinned at the teller and handed over the cash.

Who on earth would want to steal a wer-person's identity? Who could? I went as cold as the Holt Renfrew personal shopper. What about my new friend, Anton? His tales suggested to me that everyone around him was a criminal. Could he be the only honest one? What does "I work with computers" really mean in a world of oligarchs and gambling mothers?

I was so angry with myself I nearly turned skunk right there among the Chanel.

Since when had I been a victim? Never, is when. Anton could use a lesson. I'm very cognizant of my powers, but as my mater used to say, "Do not stink up a place unless you are willing to leave it forever."

In earlier times, before the advent of modern science, that was entirely true. Even now, if I'm ill or make a mistake, I've got to refill my stock of expensive 'Smell-Off'.

Once in a while, I did spray down a raccoon or a nosy dog for fun, but I hadn't sprayed a human for a century. Moderns were less likely to chase me with brooms or bullets. Vancouver was a laid-back city. Even the raccoons had rights. And I hadn't seen a human kill a bird—not even one of those noisy Canada Geese that poop everywhere—since the 1930s when food was scarce.

Part of me had gone soft on Anton. So handsome, so charming. But was he any sort of candidate for me? Scamming my credit card, ruining my rating? An identity thief?

I called my sexy Russian and arranged to meet at the Sylvia Hotel.

I lay in wait beneath the bushes on Pacific Boulevard in my natural skin, that of a raven-and-ivory mid-sized skunk. A few people walked past. A raccoon hopped down out of her tree to see what I was up to and if there was food. I threatened her with a tail-most stance. She did that chittering that raccoons do, but I raised my tail. She backed off.

Anton hopped out of a car, speaking loudly on his phone.

"But, Mama, I really like this woman. It is long past time I break up with Feodora—she bleeds me dry! And no, I will not pick you up at the casino tonight. You always stick me with the losses. Ciao!"

I stopped myself. Maybe he wasn't my thief. I scampered back to my apartment on Beach, slipped in the open window, and changed. He deserved a hearing.

I found him near the window of the Sylvia, at the Crighton memorial table named for some old Scottish drunk the bartenders loved.

My new boy was so handsome and wicked. I saw in the wall mirror that as he spoke, the waitress sighed at him. He was my tall blonde with an insane family—but at least, presumably, a human family. In 1886 I tried to pair with a wer-fox from Russia. It was a disaster of immense proportions and the cause of a massive fire in the East End. I am ashamed to this day.

But Anton? The man with the unfriendly friends? The friends who might catch and stuff me, or sell me to some horrible lab where they'd kill me with experimentation? I'm not against someone eventually trying to synthesize my long-lived genes, but I'd need a lot more trust in the regular human race to allow this.

Another part of my brain told me Anton might be redeemable, but was this just lust?

That night, I forgot my revenge plan and made love to him, and he was magic. And by that I mean not magic but very, very good. His laugh was infectious. He never took anything too seriously, but he was kind, and I was falling for him. Afterward I told him my human first name, Jeanne, so he could stop saying Lady.

We dated for a while, against my better judgement. Anton confessed that he had stolen my identity, but he provided me with a newer, better one. He even refunded Jack the money they'd taken off the platinum card.

I met Anton's mother by accident. She had come into the Sylvia Hotel to ask him for money to cover a gambling afternoon and a waiting taxi.

She took one look at me and said, "But this cannot be your new Jeanne. She is quite … normal, isn't she? Let me just say … you met Feodora? She is a model, you know. Very beautiful. And a graduate of Moscow University. His girlfriend!"

I snarled a little. The canny mother saw a flash of teeth and fur. Anton did not.

Anton pulled her away to talk in the lobby.

When he returned, he said, "I'm sorry. She doesn't know anything. I told her I broke up with Feodora."

I wondered if I should disappear. Was I in danger? How had I become so lax that I almost turned skunk in a bar in the Sylvia Hotel? What *was* stupid lust doing to me?

Mother Maria returned, visibly drunk. She drew him away from me and spoke into his ear in loud Russian whispers. Skunks have great hearing, and wers don't need translators; I always understand what is said. She called me a gypsy, and meant it as a slur.

Anton's uncle tried to convince him to move to Russia, forget me — and stay with the family business. Anton refused, saying his work was better in Canada, where he could hack more freely.

And then I had my eureka moment. Anton liked computer games, and Jack had some connections. I told Anton that I could maybe get him some legitimate work. There was just so much better to do in the human world. He laughed, but confessed to being sick of the worry. I'd never seen him worried, but that was the bravado, I guess.

I convinced him he could hack for someone on the white side of things just as easily as on the black.

In a couple of months, he was not only going downtown to his legit job — he was liking it. Goodbye to the world of hacking, gambling, and wild nights.

A waiter at the Sylvia Hotel told me that foreigners were asking about me. Perhaps Anton's family had uncovered that I was a mistress and Jack paid my bills. But, if anything, it was Feodora's overseas 'modelling' gigs that smelled suspect to me. And Mother Maria's gambling was out of control, and the oligarch was basically a crime-family kingpin. So who were they to decide that being a kept woman was a crime?

By Orthodox Easter, Mother Maria had put down her swords and invited me, Anton's official new girlfriend, to Easter lunch. Pleased, I treated myself to a new Michael Kors frock with matching purse and shoes.

It began well. None of this crowd went to church, but they sure liked to party. There were about four times as many people as Maria's west-end apartment could fit. They laughed, drank vodka at noon, and ate.

Oh, did they eat. There was borscht, sauerkraut, ham, and lamb. There were pierogies and horseradish, cabbage rolls, and all manner of side dishes made of fish and vegetables. The uncle had caviar flown in from Russia.

Mother Maria showed me a dish that was nothing but roasted garlic and onions. I looked at it, wondering if she had forgotten the meat or other vegetables.

"Jeanne," said Maria, "you must have some. Or are you, by any chance ... allergic to garlic?" She laughed loudly as she plopped some on my plate.

She hovered as I smiled genteely and ate it. Her face dropped. I looked at Anton, who was laughing and eating pierogies, unaware. Maria went back to the kitchen, clearly upset. I shrugged.

Someone had brought gifts: delicate Ukrainian Easter eggs blown out and decorated with ancient shapes. They pleased me very much. In both my forms, I love eggs.

Feodora arrived, perhaps not upset anymore at my possession of Anton. From her purse she pulled out a shiny engraved egg made entirely of silver. I'd never seen one like it.

"Oh, it is such a wonderful gift," exclaimed Mother Maria, back from the kitchen with yet another dish. "Feodora has been to Vladivostok and purchased this from an exceptional crafts-man!" She handed it to me.

I took it in my hand. Both women watched me intently as I examined it.

"How lovely," I said, "although I prefer the colourful painted eggs. Is this pure silver? Wow, how heavy." I handed it back to Feodora, who was now turning red.

Feodora threw the egg at the faux fireplace and strode out of the room, slamming the apartment door. I frowned. Again, Anton was ignoring me; he was playing cards with the men. What was wrong?

"I'm sorry," I said to Maria. "Did I offend her?"

She sniffed and turned back to the kitchen. "I need to fetch more paskha."

I smiled. That was that lovely egg bread I liked.

Suddenly, there was a young woman, with a scent different from the rest, standing beside me. She pulled me into an alcove in the hallway outside.

"You should go before they try the wooden stakes," she said.

"What?" I was astounded.

"Garlic, silver? C'mon. Don't you get it? I'm, uh, of your persuasion, kind of."

"What? Maria calls me a gypsy, but I'm not Romany of any sort."

"No, not that. Say, what do you call a group of skunks?"

She had my attention.

"A phew!" She giggled. "Name's Brenda. I work for the uncle sometimes. Watch that boy, Anton. I met you when you stalked him and almost sprayed." Her smile widened, and I saw her teeth, all pointy. Another wer! Albeit a raccoon.

"So they still hate me?"

"Yup."

"Who told them?"

"Feodora went to Russia with all your info. An old-country connection wised her up, sort of. But the wise one was a tad off. Said you were a werewolf. Crazy, eh?"

"Crazy, yes! I'm telling Anton."

"Nah, you should go. A sharpened stake will kill anything, wer or human. I don't figure these women for quitters."

"But they don't have me at all correct."

"From one mirror-wer to another, I don't want my secret out either." Brenda shook her head. "Wooden stake. Kills almost anything."

I left the apartment. It was disappointing.

All of this attempted murder! After a hard night of pacing in the park, I decided the Raccoon-girl was right. The relatives worried me now more than ever. I packed up my things, told the building manager I was moving, and disappeared to Jack's West Vancouver mansion.

I missed Anton. One day, feeling nostalgic, I went to Stanley Park in my skunk form. I wanted to see my old hunting grounds. I walked into the forest and heard the ravens making a huge ruckus.

"Traps! Evils!" they screeched. I looked around and nearly stepped on a wire noose on the ground.

I looked up to see Maria grinning at me from behind a tree. She was trapping animals.

I turned and did what any self-respecting wer-skunk would do—I raised my tail at her. She got a massive spray of lovely skunk oil all over her.

The droplets form a fine cloud, and they hold on to anything they reach. Maria was covered and screaming. Feodora emerged from behind a tree and stepped right into the cloud of scent. I laughed and pawed my little feet, then ran like the wind to a hiding place under a fallen cedar. After the screaming women left, I transformed and called 911 on my cell to report trappers in the park. Then, after mourning my Chanel suit, I put on my underthings and raced semi-naked to my car. There I put on my backup outfit and drove up the hills to Jack's house.

I saw the women that night on the six o'clock news. There they were, caught with steel traps of varying sizes in their hands, horrifying tourists. In Stanley Park! Uniformed officers from many authorities surrounded them. I giggled.

Of course, hunting in a city park is illegal. They were promptly arrested but let go soon after. Still, they must have smelled for quite a while. Meanwhile, I rested in a bath of tomatoes and lemon until I smelled fresh again.

For months, Anton searched for me, but I wasn't on social media. I didn't go to the Sylvia Hotel anymore. I still missed him, but couldn't risk the danger.

Brenda, the Raccoon-girl, passed a message along the Stanley Park wer-message system. It's very slow and like a game of broken telephone. You tell a wer, who passes it on to another wer, and so forth. Eventually, a squirrel on the North Shore chattered it to me outside Whole Foods. It sounded like Anton was offering a bag of chestnuts to a bushy-tailed girl. I shook my head at the squirrel. Dunno how that was interpreted, but Brenda found my cell number soon after and gave it to Anton.

Anton called and honestly offered to give up his awful family and stay straight. His mother and Feodora had been bundled off to Europe. The uncle didn't want their sort of publicity, and they weren't coming back. He told me he loved his new job in IT, creating games. Would I please come back to him?

I said no, regretting it, as I knew I was in love. But Jack was still alive, and I would not bond to anyone else until he was gone. Plus, I'd put out a message that I was looking for a male wer-skunk, and Anton was no skunk. I told him, through Brenda, that I wanted to have babies, but they wouldn't be with him.

A few months before he died, Jack married me. He left me the house and a whole lot of money in his will. I had a nest high up in West Van, on a huge wooded lot far from prying eyes. My future kits would be safe there. I was now secure, but bereft and alone. I cried and cried over Jack. Of all the men who'd looked after me, he was my favourite. My dreams of Anton, my Russian hacker, were done and buried like a thousand-year-old egg. And yet there was something that kept me stalking him online, wondering.

On one of my now-infrequent trips to Lost Lagoon in Stanley Park, Brenda found me almost as soon as I stepped behind a cedar to change out of my vintage Givenchy and into skunk fur.

"Howdy," she said, chewing a mouldy hoagie.

"Disgusting," I said. "Brenda."

"That's rich; you're disgusted at me? You're a scavenger just like me, no matter your fancy designer togs. Plus, you smell, you know."

"I've been around for centuries. Of course I know I smell. It is my greatest weapon."

"Look, I'm not here to fight."

"So why are you here?"

"The boy. He's sad. You know he loves you. The uncle still pays me to keep him happy and safe."

"I am also sad," I said, surprisingly honest to this wer, — who had, it is true, saved my life that Easter.

"What if we make a deal?"

"I can't see how."

"We've been studying you. Me and my pack. Don't worry, it's all hush-hush. No raccoon-wer wants the mirror-nature secret known. It's harder to hide than ever before. Now everyone has a camera on their phone. But I'm getting off topic. You, wer-skunk, you're looking for a male to procreate with, right?"

"Yes," I said, "so you see how Anton can no longer be a part of my life."

"No," said the raccoon, looking very pleased with herself. "We'll get Anton to use his hacking skills to find a male who is the same as you. I can get a bit of money out of the uncle, plus you probably have some since your mate kicked off, right? We find and pay a wer-skunk male. Between us all, we can figure out the tells. Once we find the guy, you'll get your kits like humans, with a sperm donor. Anton will be the 'father'. You'll all live happily ever after up in your West Van forest."

Brenda gave me her best toothy grin.

I hesitated. "Well, my Mater always said that wer-skunks were useless as fathers and always ran off after the babies were born. Could this actually work?"

"Yes. Then the boy will be happy as your husband and the father of the brood. Oh, and you'll agree to get the uncle to keep me and my family on the payroll, sort of permanent? Vancouver west-end rents are not cheap."

We agreed. It was, thankfully, not too hard to locate a wer-skunk male. He'd made some bad investments and was looking among the forest people for a backer for a new business. He was the perfect sire for Anton's children.

So, kits of mine, this is how I came to find and love your father, Anton, and why you never met your Russian grandmother. May she rest in peace.

I am not simply the loving suburban matron you see before you. I have a mirrored nature, and soon you will be experiencing yours as well. But Anton, your dear father, is not like us. He is all human, but he is beloved.

We wers may not know why we are as we are, moving from fur to skin, skunk to human. But as long as we enjoy our lives and do good for the universe, let us continue. Eggs for everybody!

THE SHEPHERDESS: LA TECTUME

J M Landels

JM Landels is torn between travelling the world to teach writing and swordfighting, and never leaving her idyllic farm in Langley, BC. Her debut series, fantasy bestseller Allaigna's Song: Overture, and the sequels, Aria and Chorale, are available from Pulp Literature Press and Amazon. You can follow her adventures with pen and sword at jmlandels.stiffbunnies.com.

The Shepherdess: La Tectume

Previously in The Shepherdess ...

Toinette, former shepherdess and lady's maid turned agent of the Silver Branch, has been sent to the south of France on a mission, accompanied by her hound, Jacques, her friend Luc, and his donkey Babette. Just as their destination, the Château Tectume, is within sight, they encounter Toinette's nemesis Sauvegarde and his band of dangerous cronies. In the course of escaping, Toinette kills or wounds two of them and sets fire to an inn, but she loses track of Luc and Jacques. She is captured by her sometime ally, Henri, who, misunderstandings aside, seems to have knowledge of Luc's whereabouts.

The path lifted its way along the rocky, scrub-covered hill, and the sun did the same, till we crossed from grey dawn to the full light of an orange sunrise. I paused, shielding my eyes as I turned to look back. The inferno that had been the inn had subsided, and now a thick column of black smoke tumbled upward across the clear sky. Shadow still blanketed the low ground, making it impossible to see what was happening below. Would Sauvegarde follow me and seek vengeance for Étier? Or were he and his men too busy recapturing their horses and saving the carriage? I remembered the sparks showering onto it and hoped the wretched conveyance burned to its wheels.

I turned back to the path and followed Henri as he led the captured horse around a clump of umbrella pines.

"Henri!" I exclaimed in outrage. "*Monstre!*"

I left Babette where she was and rushed to Jacques, who was sitting forlornly, leashed to a tree, his muzzle tied closed. I unmuzzled the dog, who licked my face and jumped on me in appreciation. Which prevented me from freeing Luc, who was also bound and gagged.

"How could you?" I rounded on Henri. "You brute."

The big man shrugged. "For their own safety, mademoiselle. You wouldn't want them embroiled in that." He pointed at the column of smoke.

The long and short of the story, as it finally was told, was that Luc, still unable to sleep, had heard a noise and gone to investigate. The noise had been Henri, who was skulking round the yard, lying in wait for Sauvegarde. Henri had clapped his meaty hand over Luc's mouth and frog-marched him away from the inn before he could raise an alarm. Jacques, traitor that he was, had neither barked nor growled but had happily followed Henri — expecting, no doubt, the end of a *saucisson sec.*

Henri, the consummate fool, had not questioned Luc, nor recognized Jacques. I was livid.

"How could you not recognize the animal that begged table scraps from you?" I itched to slap him, but did not quite trust I would be allowed to do so and escape retaliatory harm. And there were more important questions. "Why is Sauvegarde here? And for that matter why are you?"

"Mademoiselle," he replied solemnly, "I think I might ask the same of you."

We stared at each other for some moments while the songbirds awakened, twittering around us. His back was to the rising sun, making nothing but the whites of his eyes and his stained cravate visible. I walked three paces anti-clockwise, putting the sun at my right shoulder instead, and offered a single piece of information.

"We had stopped at the inn for the night."

"Why that inn? It's hardly welcoming."

"What others are there?" Then, before he could take the rhetorical question as part of the back and forth, "What about you?"

"I had *planned* to leave a trap for our mutual friend."

"Why?"

"That was one answer, mademoiselle. My turn now. What puts you on the road in the far south of our land with a dog, an ass, and a donkey?"

"That is more than one question. Luc and Jacques are here for my protection, and Babette to ease our load."

"I would say only one of your companions is doing her job."

I couldn't argue that point. "No thanks to you," I retorted, then repeated my previous question. "Why?"

Henri sighed. "This parry-riposte is tedious, mademoiselle." He removed his large-brimmed hat, shook it out, considered it, then placed it back upon his head. "Because he and his companions are terrible men, which I think you know first-hand. Which leads me to wonder why you would frequent the same way station."

"Ill luck." I glared at him. "I have been on the road for two months, with no thought and very little memory of those loathsome men. I fall asleep in a haystack and wake to find them surrounding me, and my companions missing ... thanks to you. It is I who have cause to be suspicious, I think." I paused, remembering the last time I'd seen Henri. "Where is Madame?"

His eyes narrowed. "I don't think I shall answer that."

Frustration boiled up my throat like mercury in an overheated glass. "Damn you, Henri! The fact that I am here at all comes down entirely to you. I would be selling perfumes in Paris had you not picked my cart out of the ditch that evening."

"Perhaps. If you had not come to Sauvegarde's notice. Or you might by lying in some other ditch. But if you'd rather be a street vendor in Paris like your flower seller here — yes, I recognize you, boy," he shot at Luc, "then why are you here?"

The frustration boiled over and I railed at him, recounting in a geyser of words all that had happened since he and Madame had left Versailles. When I finished, he said nothing but wrapped his long arm about my shoulder and pulled me into his enormous chest. His doublet smelled of wine, smoke, and less savoury things, but his arm was warm, his torso cushiony, and though I could hardly breathe, I allowed him to comfort me.

"Poor little *bergère*." He patted me on the head. "I apologize for saving your life not once, but thrice."

I started to pull away, if only to point out I had saved his as well, but he kept me in the suffocating embrace. "But now, I really do need that letter opener back."

I elbowed him in the ribs — right at the point I'd once sewn up a bullet wound. Sadly, it had healed long ago and was no more sensitive than the rest of his expansive flank. "Have you followed me all the way for that?" I asked.

"Not at all. You only just now revealed that you have it."

Luc, who had been tending Babette while listening to this exchange, spoke up at last. "Milady has no letter opener save this."

I turned within Henri's still-tight embrace to see Luc pointing the wavering end of a rapier at Henri's ribs. "Unhand her."

Henri gave a mighty sigh, then batted the sword away with his gloved hand. He released me with a shove that sent me stumbling toward Luc. Luc stepped around me, and in that moment Henri grasped the blade of the rapier and lifted it from Luc's hand as easily as plucking a marguerite. He tossed the sword back into Babette's cart and sank down to rest on his haunches.

"What am I to do with you two?" he asked. "It would be a comedy, but it's not likely to end in marriages. Michel thinks I have the letter opener. Sauvegarde thinks Maeve has it, and I thought Sauvegarde had it, while you've been wandering the countryside with it all along."

"I *had* it," I said at last, still wondering what part of my tale had given that away. "But no longer," I lied. "I left it in Paris."

"Mon Dieu," he swore. "Is there no end to the trouble you've caused? Where? Do not say Maeve's house. That has been searched."

Down to the poison cabinet? I wondered. No matter. "It is with someone I trust. But I will reveal their location only to Madame."

Surprisingly, he said, "*Bon.* That is good enough for me. We'd best get moving."

Our destination and Henri's turned out to be the same: the Château Tectume. But instead of the road that meandered around and back across the southwest face of the forbidding mountain, we took a network of goat trails through the tangled and stunted forest that covered the northeast flank. Each juncture we took was marked, most often by yellow flowers but sometimes with a fading yellow silk ribbon caught in the branches of a tree and once, in a barren, rocky stretch, by pale freckles of paint splashed across a large rock, as if an artist had flicked her paintbrush there. These signs were subtle and casual, and I would not have noticed them at all if Henri had not been looking for them so intently.

The paths were barely wide enough for Henri, and Luc often had to lift the end of Babette's cart to navigate roots, washouts, and stretches where only one wheel fit upon the track. The track was too precarious to ascend mounted, so I led Marteau while Henri took charge of the fiery stallion who had adopted Babette. Marteau was, after all, half my horse, and he seemed glad enough to see me after carrying Henri all these miles.

The trees thinned, but the path became more precarious — cut in some places from smooth granite, with bare stone cliffs to one side and a precipitous drop to the forest below. Luc, who hardly ever complained, was grumbling.

"Would not the road have been easier?"

"Easier but more dangerous," Henri replied. "Sauvegarde still has horses, and we can only move as fast as our feet and your ass." This was true. Henri was too heavy for the delicate little stallion, and I wouldn't hazard the animal's temper.

"Why would he venture to the château?" I asked. "He was clearly lying in wait for someone." I paused, remembering the landlord's intent to light a signal.

Henri completed my thought. "If his victim was warned off by the conflagration at the inn, what might his recourse be?"

"Pursue them up the road. The higher the road goes, the slower the travel. And the pursuers catch up with fresher horses that have not just ridden the descent," I finished. "But who is Sauvegarde after?"

Henri looked down his amused chin at me. "You truly don't know? Maeve."

It made sense, like turning over a tapestry that one had only seen from the reverse, and seeing the knots and tufts of colours transform to images. But only one corner had been folded back, and I still could not see the whole.

"Why would Madame be coming to that godforsaken inn? Who is she meeting?"

Henri looked even more surprised. "Me, of course."

This was exasperating. "If she's been staying at La Tectume, why not meet there?"

"Why, to save me this benighted climb."

That was all the unsatisfactory answer I could glean for the moment as we navigated a particularly perilous section of trail. The stallion's hind hoof slid, sending a shower of rocks tumbling off the cliff to take flight above the eagles who circled below us.

Once the path widened and my heart slowed, I spoke again. "That means Madame is in danger of being overtaken by those vile men. Should we not have ridden to her aid?"

Henri turned a patronizing smile upon me. "Gallant little *bergère*, Maeve is not without her defences, and we would do well to stay out of the way of them. Your conflagration is all the warning she'll need."

The trail turned downward, in toward the heart of the mountain then back out and up again, the brief respite lost in another steep upward climb. We rounded the promontory and were bitten in the face by the cold March wind that scoured the exposed flank. I thought about the season, with flowers blooming but winds still cold, and hoped it was still too early for ticks, given the brush we'd walked through. That thought sent my ankles and armpits itching with imaginary bloodsuckers, until a rumbling crash shook the mountain and sent the stallion skittering back into me. Only my hand on Marteau's reins stopped me from falling over the edge as the steady gelding braced his neck, pinned his ears, and held his ground. I recovered my footing, wrapping an arm around Marteau's neck for security.

"What was that?" I squeaked, my voice strangled by the pounding of my pulse.

A cloud of dust rose from ahead. Henri beckoned me forward, and I followed another twenty yards along the path, my nerves as frayed as those of the stallion, who now danced a dangerous jig in front of me. A clearing in the trees showed the road below us — and a fresh wound of bare earth in the landscape where rock had tumbled down to cover it.

"Is that one of her defences?" I asked.

Henri nodded slowly. "Most likely. Now we need only hope that Sauvegarde is on the right side of it — or even better, underneath."

Night had fallen once more, and the last hour of our climb was more perilous than the other hours put together, illuminated as it was by only half a moon. But at last the trail broke into the wider road and made the last quarter mile safer, if no less tiring.

Finally we met the twin towers of the outer bailey: squat round things, for the landscape gave them all the height they needed. The bridge over the dry moat was raised.

Henri cupped his hands around his mouth and bellowed toward the gatehouse. "Ho there! Three travellers in need of sanctuary stand before you."

A boy's voice, not yet broken, replied. "State your names."

"Henri Fabron, and these are my servants."

"Let them speak for themselves."

I cleared my throat uneasily. "Antoinette Berger," I called, then elbowed Luc to follow suit.

"And your business," came back the voice when Luc had announced himself.

"I have a meeting with the Countess," replied Henri, his patience thinning.

"You're late," came another voice, one I knew well and had sorely missed these several months.

With a creak and a grumble, the chains in the bridge began to let out, one clanking link at a time, until the narrow drawbridge thudded to the ground at our feet.

Henri had to blindfold the stallion to lead him across, and Marteau was none too happy either, but he followed the phlegmatic Babette willingly enough. Once we were across, the bridge began to rise behind us. I noticed with unease that a portcullis, invisible from the other side in the inky night, still separated us from the inner bailey, trapping us between it and the closing bridge. I looked up and saw what I had only ever heard of before: murder holes. Two of them let in the feeble light of the moon.

At last the portcullis made its equally noisy ascent, and we walked into the no-man's land between walls. I caught the familiar smell of sheep and saw white splotches dotted here and there across surprisingly grassy hillocks between the inner and outer walls.

There was a clatter, and the gatehouse door opened beside us. A small man, wearing a breastplate that shone white in the moonlight, stepped out and, hands on hips, looked up at the towering face of Henri.

"Catrin!" exclaimed Henri, and embraced Madame — for the small armoured man was she — in the French, Provençal, and Italian manner for good measure. He stepped back and slapped her on the cuirass with a ringing sound. "You're not nearly as soft as you ought to be."

"And you, Henri, are as rude as ever." She stepped around him. "Toinette, is that really you?" Then she took me entirely off guard by kissing me on both cheeks in a shocking display of equity. "It is so very good to see you alive and well, chick."

We followed Madame along the causeway between the two gatehouses. I felt as if I were in one of Ahmed's romances from the days of Marie de France, following this strange lady-knight through a mediaeval château fort.

When the animals had been stabled, Madame led us to the kitchen, which was bustling with post-prandial cleanup, and secured us bread, cheese, and cold mutton. We sat next to the scullery, and when we'd had a few bites of food and a sip, or in Henri's case a slosh, of good red wine, Madame reiterated, "You're late."

Henri shrugged. "I was delayed on the road."

Her look was dark. "Had I not seen the signal fire, I would have ridden into Sauvegarde's trap. You were supposed to divert them."

"That was no signal. That was Toinette setting fire to the inn."

She leaned back against the wall, startled, then sat upright again as the cuirass dug into her. "And what of Gradi?"

"The innkeeper?" Henri asked.

"Shot," I answered, finding my voice at last. "In the back as he tried to flee."

"The monsters. Hanging is too good for them."

"Étier won't even get that," I said in a dull voice. "And perhaps not Louis-Auguste either." I felt calm, dead calm, and yet could not understand why my eyes were streaming and my shoulders shaking as I looked at the dried blood on my skirts.

The first thing I did after shedding my mud- and blood-caked clothing was sleep. The last time I had closed my eyes, they opened to the muzzle of an arquebus, which made me think I might never be able to slide into easy unconsciousness again. But slide I did, beneath the memory hanging over me, so that my eyes had barely time to close before exhaustion dropped me like a stone into its deep well.

It was the dead of night when I woke. Blue moonlight was filtering through the cracks in ancient shutters that only partially blocked the icy wind singing around the château. A warm sigh from behind me shocked me into stillness. I barely dared breathe. Though when I did at last, I recognized Madame's perfume. The bed was hers.

With the same stealth I had used when extricating myself from the family bed to start the morning bread without waking my siblings, I eased out from under the covers. My skin prickled with the cold of the room. Even my shift was filthy, and so I had gone to bed as naked as a ratling.

I felt beneath the bed till my fingers encountered the handle of the chamber pot. No delicate porcelain like the pots in Versailles or Paris, this was beaten tin, and I winced at the clatter it made as I dragged it out. That noise was nothing to the thundering of my piss as it filled the pot, unmuffled by skirts or shift, but Madame did not stir.

As I waited for the interminable stream of urine to end, I felt a familiar ache between my hipbones, and touched a finger to my quoynt. Sure enough, it came away dark, even by the scant moonlight.

I was colder now, my teeth chattering as I fumbled my way to the basin and ewer of water by the window. I washed as quietly as I could, then searched for my clothing. I couldn't crawl back into bed with Madame like this. I found my shift, already soiled with Étier's blood, and stuffed it between my legs. Making a nest with the rest of my filthy skirts, I pulled my travelling cloak over me and curled up there till dawn.

When I awoke again I was still cold, though someone had lit a fire in the hearth and opened the shutters so spring sunshine flooded the room. I unlocked my aching joints and rolled to my knees, feeling the warm gush of blood onto my already-ruined shift. No matter. I saw the happiest sight I could hope for: a large copper basin, standing in the sunlight, glowing like a small sun itself, with clean white cloths draped over its side. Beside it was a pail of water, and on the hook over the fire, a gently steaming kettle. There was not much water in either — the well in this high arid place must have a long hard draw — but there was enough.

I washed my hands and face in the basin first, dumped that water into the copper tub, then added more from the kettle. It was just enough to cover my ankles when I stepped in, and my hips when I folded myself and sat down. I rested there a few decadent minutes, feeling warmth soothe my aches, before setting to work with the scrub brush and a fine hard block of Marseilles soap.

When the water had no heat left I stood, letting the sunlight and the wind — warmer now — take the moisture from my skin. I felt blissful and pure. That is, until my eyes fell once more on the heap of filthy clothes on the floor. I cast around the room for my spare skirt, shift, and blouse before remembering that I'd left all that in Babette's cart.

But there was a clean shift, blouse, skirt, and bodice lying on the bed. They must have been for me, for I couldn't imagine Madame in anything so plain. I donned them, took one of the fresh towels as my clout, and set to work laundering: soaking my clothes in the hand basin first, then dumping them in the tepid remains of my bath water. As I was transferring the last of these to the tub, there was a knock on the door.

"Oh!" said a red-faced maid, who had clearly just climbed many stairs very quickly. "That's my job, Madame." She put down a tray of bread, milk, and what smelled enticingly like coffee, then curtsied. "The general says have your breakfast then join her in the solar when you're done."

Bewildered, I sat on the edge of the bed and poured myself some milk and coffee, wondering if the poor girl had mistaken me for someone else.

With hasty mouthfuls transferred to my belly I arose, leaving the tray for the maid and feeling guilty for that. Nervous about meeting this general, I peered into the polished brass mirror — no Versailles glass here — and tidied my hair beneath my cap. I smoothed my kirtle and double-checked my hands and face for any last speck of blood or mud.

The maid had left no clue as to where the solar was, and being utterly unfamiliar with the usual anatomy of châteaux forts, I had no choice but to enter the great hall and cast about for someone to ask. It was midmorning, and the hall was empty, the hearth cold. I paused here for a breath, taking in the high-raftered ceilings and the whitewashed stone walls skirted with bright tapestries. The pale colours soothed my eyes, and the clean air my lungs. Such a contrast to the glittering opulence and foetid stench of perfume and sweat that cloyed the ballroom of Versailles.

Rushed though I was, I paused to peer at the tapestries as I went. They seemed to tell a story, starting at the east entrance and wrapping the hall. And they seemed old. Horses, knights, queens, and catapults from an earlier age. Not just warriors, but farmers, gardeners, and craftsmen appeared in the scenes. I reached out to touch the white knots that formed the woolly back of a lamb cradled in a shepherdess's arms.

"Please do not touch it, mademoiselle," came a voice from behind me.

I jerked my hand back and turned to see a lad with an arm-load of firewood walk past. He let the logs tumble beside the hearth, wiped his hands on his braies, and turned toward me. "It's over five hundred years old, and we only bring it out when the leaders are in residence."

The boy's face left me speechless. It was scarred on one side, the flesh puckered and twisted, partially obscured by the long black braid that hung down over his right shoulder, ending at his — no, her — quite obvious bosom. That should not have shocked me, for I'd worn breeches before. But only to disguise myself as a boy. This woman was not in disguise.

At last I found my tongue and mumbled an apology, curtsying out of habit. "Where might I find the solar?" I asked at last.

"Through that door, left up the stairs," she said, then added as I started to thank her, "Caustic lye. My former husband threw it in my face. Since you were wondering."

"I ... I'm so sorry."

"Don't be. He's the one with the devil's fork up his arse now, and we're all better for it."

Not knowing what else to say, I curtsied again and hastened out the portal she'd indicated.

There were only a handful of stairs and then a wooden door. I assayed it with a timid knock.

"Enter," came the clear voice of Madame. I breathed a sigh of relief, knowing I would not be alone with the general.

Alone I was not. The door opened into a sunny room with many glazed windows — the first glass I'd seen here. A dozen chairs with thick upholstery, and many more embroidered cushions, studded the white wool carpet. Scattered on those chairs and cushions were half a dozen women.

Madame arose from her chair and crossed the room, taking both my hands and kissing me on each cheek. "Bienvenue, Toinette. I trust you are well rested?"

She still had my hands, and it seemed rude to withdraw them, so I bobbed my knees in a half curtsy. Her fingers tightened on mine and restrained my dip. "We do not curtsy in here, Toinette," she whispered before leading me by the hand to the circle of women. "Please, take a seat."

Two of the women were seated on the floor, one tailor-style and embroidering on a hoop, the other resting her back against the outside wall, her trousered legs stretched out in front of her. The other three were in chairs: one reading a worn-looking book, the other two in deep conversation over tiny cups of strong-smelling coffee. I chose a chair away from them, and not next to the one Madame had reclaimed.

"Help yourself." She indicated a low table in the middle of the haphazard circle, laden with fruit, cheese, coffee, and wine. Then she clapped her hands. "My friends, now that we are all here, please allow me to introduce Antoinette Bergère. This young woman has been on a remarkable and perilous journey, which we will hear about in due course."

The needleworker put down her hoop and looked up at me with a pretty smile. "Is it true you slaughtered that animal Pedro Étier?"

The trousered woman sat up and looked me square in the face. "Oh, bravo, young lady. You haff done us all a service." She had a strange accent—a bit like that of the Duchesse d'Orléans, but stronger. Like all the women here, she was unwigged, and her light brown hair was liberally streaked with grey and held back by a blue ribbon that matched her pale eyes.

One of the coffee drinkers put down her cup and appraised me. She had a small red dot painted between her brows, and her strangely straight-cut emerald gown was brighter and more gold-laden than Versailles itself. She seemed about to say something.

"Barroom tales later," interrupted Madame. "We have strategy to discuss."

"So," said the pale-eyed woman. "Vill it be siege, do you think?"

"I'm not sure," said Madame, frowning into her cup. "An army massing below would call attention, even in this abandoned part of the rôyaume. And I don't think Sauvegarde has an army at his disposal."

"But Louis does," responded the pale-eyed woman.

"If he were willing to send armies against us," said a matronly woman, "he wouldn't waste good cash on that scoundrel Sauvegarde."

The colourfully garbed one shrugged. "Whether there is an army there or not," she said in a musical accent, "we are still behind a rockslide, with no way of getting your carriage down, Kristina."

The older woman waved a dismissive hand. "I can ride."

"I cannot," said the matron.

The needleworker tipped her pretty chin and smiled. "It's only a matter of sitting on the saddle with a leg on each side—or both on one if you prefer forks."

The matron looked down her nose. "Can you see me perched on one of those top-heavy beasts, tottering down the mountainside? I have not learned to ride yet and I have no intention of doing so now."

"Well," said Kristina, "I must go without you then. It is a long journey back to Rome."

"Take Henri with you," said Madame. "He makes a partway-useful bodyguard, and his size alone prevents much."

Kristina smiled. "Be careful, Maeve, I may just keep him. A blackamoor in my kingdom would prove a fine distraction to keep the empty heads gossiping."

"Henri is like a stray cat. He stays as long as it pleases him. But he will at least get you out of this barren place. Now, Toinette—please tell your story to these fine women."

I was caught off guard, my mouth partly full of a cream pastry. I blotted my lips, swallowing too fast. At last, I was able to mumble, "Which story, Madame?"

"All of it, my dear. From the time you left your home, till now."

The sunshine through the windows had crept all the way across the floor by the time I had finished.

"You left out a part," said Madame. "Your meeting with the Dame de Paris."

I met her eyes with no small amount of guilt.

"Excellent," said the green-garbed woman. She shook her head and her gold earrings tinkled accompaniment to her musical voice. "I could not find the gap in your story. Was it when you were at Versailles, or later, in Paris?"

I glanced at Madame.

"You may speak freely here, Toinette. We are all sisters, and you have just passed your first test admirably. You may transmit her message."

"And the mot de clé?" I asked.

"*Renoncule*," she replied.

I nodded, relief uncoiling in my belly. "She came to our house in Paris and instructed me to bring a message to the mistress of La Tectume. I had no idea that was you, Madame." A slight accusatory tone seeped into my voice, and I quelled it. "But the message, it makes no sense. 'To Scarron King.'"

Silence filled the room. I opened my mouth to say more, but what could I add to these scant nonsensical words I'd carried the length of France?

"Ah," said the woman with the book, who had been silent thus far. She placed a navy blue ribbon between the pages, smoothed it with a deliberate hand, and folded the book closed. "So soon."

She closed her eyes, and the room returned to an almost reverent silence. When she opened her eyes again, her face was businesslike. "So, Kristina, it seems I must leave with you."

"And can you ride, Françoise?" asked Madame.

"Indeed I cannot, but I shall learn on the way."

I admired the determined set of her chin. The tortuous route down the mountain was no easy road on which to learn.

"You will need dresses … and jewels. Mathilde and Marie-Claude are still at Versailles," said my mistress. "They can lend you some of mine."

"No." Françoise shook her head. "That is not the approach I

shall take. For one, I think it better for you and me that Louis makes no connection between us. But I cannot compete with the Soissons, la Montespan, or you in beauty. Instead I shall appeal to his conscience."

"If the man still has one," interrupted the matron.

"If he does not, I shall not succeed in any case. He was brought up by Mazarin, and godliness lies within his soul, waiting to bloom."

"That is a perilous path," said the brightly dressed woman. "A godly man is harder to steer than a lascivious one."

"That is true. But it is my only path to his heart. The man is sated with carnality—he has dined on this rich fare too long, and craves cool water."

At that moment there was a frantic pounding on the solar door. The women glanced at one another, straightened their skirts, and the two on the floor rose to take chairs.

"Toinette, please see who that is," said Madame.

It was Luc, red in the face and out of breath. "Henri sent me," he panted. "There are men . . . moving up the north path."

Madame stood. "Well, the path is narrow and defensible. A few well-placed musket balls and crossbow bolts should defend it."

"How many balls and bolts do you have, Madame?" asked Luc. "There are at least a hundred men down there."

Kristina stood, smiling. "You mean I'll have to fight my way down? How delightful."

"We'll do nothing of the sort," said Françoise. "We cannot afford to risk you to a stray arrow or a simple misstep off the side of the mountain. You are the only sovereign amongst us, and until I have finished my task, the only one with access to heads of states."

"Except Louise," said the youngest woman.

"No longer," said Maeve, "but that is a tale for another time. I agree with Françoise. You are here till we clear this place of threat. Boy, tell Henri to notify the captain of the guard. Toinette … with me."

Once in Madame's chamber—so different from her opulent ones at Versailles and Paris—I received an instant lesson in valeting as I helped buckle her cuisses, cuirass, gorget, and pauldrons.

"Never mind the lower legs," she said. "I have no intention of appearing past the parapets."

Last came the helm, visor hooked in the open position. I knew nothing of the armour of warfare, but I felt this harness must exist for show rather than battle. The black-and-gold enamel decorations were intricate and showed no sign of hard use.

This ornate armour was in contrast to Kristina's. We met the woman in the stairwell. She was dressed head to toe in plain steel harness, dented and dusty.

"Kristina, you cannot be seen out there," insisted Madame. "Sauvegarde does not know you are here, and there is no advantage in revealing that hand."

"And who will know it is I?" challenged the diminutive woman.

"Tell me you were not planning to draw that." Madame pointed at the short arming sword hanging from Kristina's waist. "You will come with me to the battlements if you must, but stand well back, with your visor down. Do not make me order you, Kristina."

What I saw next didn't strike me so much then as it would years later, with decades of politics under my belt. The former Queen of Sweden bent a knee to my mistress.

I followed Madame and the Swedish queen up the narrow stair that led to the top of the curtain wall, them in their armour, me in my plain grey borrowed kirtle. I was a wren caught between two eagles. As we reached the top, Madame turned to me.

"Stand here, Toinette. Do not be tempted to show your bare head above the battlements. But listen well, and remember every word. Commit them to exact memory, and if aught should go awry, run to Henri in the gatehouse and Madame de Scarron within the hall and repeat all to them."

"Awry?" I asked. "How will I know what awry might look like?"

She smiled at me fondly. "If Kristina and I cannot tell them ourselves, chérie."

She strode out to the edge of the battlement, and Kristina took up a position halfway between us, her visor down, looking every bit the part of a fairy-tale knight. Madame put the coiled trumpet to her lips and blew a single long note. It felt as if even the birds and the wind on that craggy peak stopped to listen.

"Show yourselves," called Madame, and waited. She put both hands on the wall and leaned forward. "You cannot take this château by force."

I mouthed her words after her, trying to burn them in my memory. Another pause.

"That we have not yet begun potting you like pigeons is an act of forbearance."

More silence, that not even the wind answered.

"Gwyn," she said more quietly, turning to face the archer at the neighbouring tower. "Take the feather from that one's hat."

An arrow sang through the quiet air. There was a distant sound, like the bleat of a lamb, a clatter of rocks, and a curse. A lone rock echoed its bouncing way down the cliff.

"Apologies, Denis," called Madame. "I asked my archer to take your feather, not the whole hat and wig besides. But accidents happen."

"I have two hundred men at my disposal, Catherine," came the snarling voice I recognized as Sauvegarde's. "We may not be able to storm your walls, but we can starve you out."

She laughed musically, like a comedienne in a play. "How long are you prepared to sit on a barren hillside? We are fully stocked within these walls, and our well is deep. How many provisions did *you* carry up the mountain?"

She turned to Gwyn again. "The one beside him. In the leg."

There was the sound of a steel-tipped arrow punching through metal, and a full-out yell.

"We'd rather you left on your own feet, Sauvegarde, but we'll leave you for the eagles if need be. Ten. Nine. Eight ..." There were more sounds of rocks falling. "Seven. Six." Madame waved at Gwyn, who sent another arrow that caused a second yell and more rocks. "Five. Four. Three." The last two she said in a conversational voice: "Two and one. That buys us space," she said, turning from the parapet, "but gains us no time."

"What does he hope to achieve?" said Kristina, lifting her visor as the pair strode toward me.

"Delay, and nothing more. We must get Scarron to Versailles, or all this crumbles."

"How does he know that?" Kristina asked as I followed them back down the stairs.

"He doesn't—I think. But either he knows you're here, or he thinks the letter opener is." Madame's glance fell briefly across mine. "And he would take either to his master."

Kristina snorted. "He would have a hard time taking me."

Madame paused on the staircase, looking up at the diminutive former sovereign. "I don't think he needs all of you. Your head would do."

Kristina shrugged. "Still hard."

I admired the woman's bravery, but Madame frowned. "You may dress, and ride to battle, and even love like a man, but you are still half the height and a third the weight of a man like Henri. Sauvegarde and his three companions are the most ruthless, least moral men I have ever had the misfortune to know. Do not underestimate them, Kristina."

"Two," I said softly. "Two companions. Étier's dead."

Madame turned on the stair once more and wrapped her arms around me. "My dear, I am so sorry. We should not have forgotten your incredible feat."

It was not a soft embrace between Madame's cuirass and plated arms, but I felt I could not respectfully break from it. Kristina rescued me.

"How did you do it?" she asked. "We never got that story."

"Uh … he fell on the sword I was carrying."

She clapped me on the back so hard I nearly fell down the stair. "I'm sure there's more to it than that, sister. You must tell me all … over a beer."

By the time we reached the bottom of the stairwell, my stomach was in turmoil. *You must tell me all*, the Queen had said, and until that moment my thoughts had not fully encompassed 'all'.

Despite the fact I had climbed a mountain while covered in Étier's blood, I had set aside the memory of how that blood had vomited out of his dying mouth onto me. I had butchered plenty of sheep in my time and been spattered in blood from dawn to dusk. The smell and sight held no weight for me, and that was how I had worn Étier's all day. It had been an inconsequential part of my attire.

But now, the prospect of retelling it, of reawakening the memory, made me shake like a newborn lamb on a windy day. As we stepped into the sunbaked yard, the heat and light assaulted my eyes and made me sneeze. And then I emptied my stomach onto the packed earth, spattering the hem of my skirt and Madame's kidskin boots.

I had not time to apologize before Jacques bounded over, wagging and wriggling like a puppy to lick my face and then turn with intent to my stomach contents shining in the sunlight.

"No, Jacques," I moaned, trying to drag him away by the scruff of his neck.

"Leave him be, mamselle," came Henri's voice from behind us. "Unless you want to shovel it up yourself."

I wiped my mouth with the back of my sleeve and turned to glare at Henri. Ire at the big man happily replaced the nausea. "In that case, he can sleep at the foot of *your* bed tonight," I snapped.

"Madame, Majesté." I curtsied to the two women. "Forgive me, please. Have I your leave to go?"

Madame put her gloved fingers under my chin and looked me in the eye. "Are you ill or pregnant, my dear?"

"Neither," I stammered.

"I think," said Kristina, folding her plated arms across her cuirass, "she has only just realized she killed a man. Am I right, sparrow?"

"Ahh," said Madame and kissed me upon my sweating brow. "Go and wash, my dear. But we will talk, and soon."

I nodded and felt the ground sway beneath me as I stepped toward the staircase. I paused, my hand on the lintel, leaning on it for support more than I would like. "Could someone direct me to the chamber I was in?" I asked. "I can't quite remember the way."

Instead of answering, Henri strode toward me and, as if I weighed no more than a lamb at castrating time, scooped me up in his arms. "I'll take you there, mamselle. You look too white to walk."

I kicked, furious at the indignity and yet totally ineffectual in my protest. "Put me down, you brute!" I hissed.

"Stop squirming, or I'll put you over my shoulder."

"And I'll throw up down your back."

"So stop squirming, or you'll be washing my clothes as well as your own."

Defeated, I closed my eyes and held still, but in no way relaxed, as he carried me and his own bulk up the staircase to Madame's chambers.

When I had washed my face, wiped my boots, and rinsed the hem of my skirt, I found Henri sitting in a chair outside the door.

"Don't you have more important things to do?" I asked with more acid in my voice than strictly necessary.

"Me? No. The general and her women have important things to do. I just wait for orders."

"By 'general', do you mean Madame?"

He lifted his fuzzy caterpillar eyebrows. "And here I thought you were in the inner circle."

"Am I?"

"Aren't you? You've been in their embroidery clique, which is more than I ever have."

I felt lost, bewildered, and — as usual when Henri was at hand — angry. "If I'd never met you, how simple my life would have been," I growled. "What ill luck put you on my path that night?"

"If I hadn't been on your path, would you have continued on to Paris after Sauvegarde ran you into a ditch? I would say it was Sauvegarde who was the ill luck, not I."

I couldn't argue with that. I may have persevered and tried to make my life as a merchant in Paris, or I may have turned tail and slunk home, like a dog caught in the henyard. But neither life would have taken me to the court of the Sun King, or to this château fort in the Languedoc with blood on my hands.

"Though," he said, interrupting my musing, "I was the reason Sauvegarde was on the road. And so if I hadn't been following him … well. I guess you may blame me after all."

I gave him my darkest glare as I swept past on my way down the stairs. "Do not tempt me, Henri."

§

Find out what happens next in Issue 42, Spring 2024. For past adventures of the Shepherdess, check out even-numbered issues of Pulp Literature *from Issue 24 onward.*

Now Available!

The magical conclusion to the must-read epic trilogy

the adventures of Allaigna sing

simply a joy to read

keeps you turning pages from beginning to end

an immensely satisfying epic

PULPLITERATURE.COM/ALLAIGNAS-

THE ETERNITY MACHINE

Graham J Darling

Ottawa neo-alchemist **Graham J Darling** has bred hybrids of disruptive SF, mythopoeic fantasy, and unearthly horror for Frivolous Comma and Sword & Mythos. *His story 'A Pleasant Walk, A Pleasant Talk' appeared in* Pulp Literature Issue 21, Winter 2019. 'The Eternity Machine' *originally appeared in* Dark Matter Magazine Issue 006. Graham *has recently completed his debut novel, the high/hard/dark fantasy* Fallen World. *Visit him at* fiction.grahamjdarling.com.

The Eternity Machine

History is for survivors. But if I'm to help you grasp what we went through that terrible night, and what you all face now, then best we take this in tiny steps, just as it happened to me.

Like a baby dropped from its mother's arms, I screamed, that moment I lost the touch of the Earth.

Twisting and flailing in a howling wind, I felt my outstretched fingers scrape something huge, my bare foot kick away a small, soft body, all falling with me. I was blind, suffocating in the bedsheets that had wound around my head and tightened as I tumbled and twirled.

There'd been an explosion, too, like a thunderclap at my window. Its echoes, mixed with snaps and groans, as if the building around me were coming apart, seemed now a physical fluid filling my ears to near bursting. But this agonizing pressure, presently, my stifled shrieks seemed to relieve, as the roar of rushing air subsided to a moan, then a sigh. Until at last, except for my own pants and sobs and the occasional distant creak and rumble, I found myself floating in dead silence and perfect stillness — and, when I had torn the last of the clinging fabric from my face, utter darkness. My outer senses no longer found cause for alarm, but I was still falling inside.

I tasted blood. My nose was filling with blood. Another minute of panic as I learned to deal with bodily fluids that no longer drained on their own.

As my battered wits recovered, I saw a luminous dot drift by, and grabbed at it. It was the phosphorescent ON button of my television remote. There was no sign anywhere of my glowing clock or the other usual night lights of my room, or light from the street outside.

I flinched from a rustle at my ear — felt there a well-thumbed textbook slowly fan open like a night-blooming flower. I groped further, met a rough surface I guessed was my stucco ceiling, pushed off that. Moved through a cloud of other books, clothing, clean and dirty dishes, a solitary Christmas card. Bumped into my wastebasket, clambered around my desk. Found and opened the bathroom door, then quickly shut it again. Followed an electric umbilical to the foetal refrigerator.

Another glowing spot appeared, which grew into a shining line: the crack at the threshold of my apartment, coming into view as I came around a corner, through which sweet light beckoned from the hallway beyond.

I reached my front door and pulled it open, then started at the apparition before me: bloody, haggard, levitating, hair on end, like a murdered man's ghost come back to assure his lady, by looks alone, that only horror awaits beyond the grave.

It was my own reflection, where none had ever been.

Awestruck, I extended a hand without thinking. At arm's length, my fingers met a strange, frictionless surface that exactly returned my hand's warmth and pressure. In the dim emergency lighting, the monstrous mirror stretched away on every side as far as I could see — like a titan's polished cleaver that had chopped the building in two — and then slightly slid apart the halves, for in front was a gap in both floor and ceiling through which I glimpsed other lit stories, and blackness, beyond.

I grew aware of a whisper around me and a new breeze at my back. Socks and papers flowed by from behind; I saw the narrow abyss suck them past its carpeted brink; felt it pull at me as well. In sudden panic, I threw myself back, and the door slammed shut.

I collided with something springy yet fixed. Feeling around, I found it was my garage-sale sofa, firmly lodged in my shattered window. I clung and shivered, and strained to hear any sign of my neighbours.

It was that dead spell between Yule and New Year when nothing gets done, like the unlucky epagomenal days of Pharaonic Egypt, when the calendar has run out and humanity holds its breath, its life in the balance, until the Nile surges to water the desert and Time begins again. Most of the other undergrads were gone for the holidays — those who had somewhere to go — and the rez stood largely empty. I had locked myself in for the duration with Livy and Thucydides, searching the past to explain the present and prepare for the future.

To explain and prepare for … this?

As I held still, the air around me grew hot and stale. It reminded me of long-ago nights when, buried in blankets, I'd hide from the ghosts of sabre-tooths prowling for cave-child flesh, or listen to the mystery of my own heartbeat and imagine great armies marching, marching through the night.

The building creaked some more then went quiet again.

There came a flickering light and faint noise from beyond the couch. I shifted around — the air turned cooler and fresher — and peered through a chink at the world outside.

Feebly lit, the familiar towers of the campus now leaned, cracked and windowless, at strange angles. A couple had come free from their foundations, held to the earth only by bared roots of pipes and wires; one had gone missing. Banks of snow, shaken loose, floated about as solid clouds.

The light, I could now see, came from the crumpled wreck of an automobile slowly drifting by, burning. The sounds, I could now hear, came from the people still trapped inside and, away in the distance, the slow tolling of a great bell.

Its every stroke rang impossibly long. There seemed nothing I could do; I turned away. After a while, I went back to the fridge and, with practice, managed to squeeze some of the contents of a plastic bottle into my mouth.

The light outside dimmed, the screaming died away, but the bell tolled on. Eventually, adrenaline abated; exhaustion set in ...

A piercing whistle roused me from outside the window. A girl was floating there.

She bore a bike lamp on her brow. Her triangular wings had been diagonally cut from a college flag, their corners fastened to her feet and to the broomsticks in her hands. Her hair was tied back in a waving ponytail. She had swim goggles on and a scarf wrapped over her nose and mouth. From the scarf's coils poked the whistle she held in her teeth as she spoke to me.

"Hey in there!" she said. "Hello? My name's Ann."

"Ned," I said, blinking. "I'm Ned. You're ... So there's ..."

"Ned, is anyone else with you, or nearby?"

"Just me here. But a car passed a while ago ..."

She asked for a description, and I gave it. "I think we found that one, but I'll check," she said.

"Ann, please … what's happened?"

"We're having a meeting to talk about that. Whatever it is, it looks bad—we must be brave. I need you to get dressed and pack all the food and clean water you can find. Protect your eyes and breathe through cloth—there's a lot of broken glass in the air out here. I'll be back for you soon."

"Don't …!" I said, and then, "All right. Soon."

I loaded a knapsack and rigged a mask from a T-shirt and plastic wrap while she checked other nearby apartments. Then she threw me the end of the towline tied to her waist.

Conserving her battery, Ann mostly guided herself, bat-like, by the echoes of her whistle and the call of the bell. In the odd flash, I saw us pass between huge, deformed structures. They seemed no longer of human make: monstrous corals, morels, stalagmites—or stalactites—it was impossible to tell anymore.

She left me at a steeple with a "Here you are. Good luck!" and flew off to her next rescue.

A gruff old man in an antique gas mask (his name was Bert) was anchored there. Between hammer blows on the bell's bronze lip every minute or so, he added me as a knot to his string, then guided me within. I followed a rope through a tunnel of stairs.

Inside the church, the stained glass had blown out like all the other windows, but the remaining naked strips of lead still told their stories in outline. So did much else here continue to pretend at normal: the pews bolted to the tiled floor, the congregation jammed into the pews. There were night workers, and resident students like me, and families from the edge of a nearby housing project nicked by a new reflective wall on that side, too. Here and there, a light showed briefly as someone compulsively checked their phone but found no signal from the unpowered network; those glimmers slowed and ceased as hopes and charges faded.

Lovers whispered, babies nursed, others of us snored or cried or softly sang. And all the while, with bulletins and song sheets, we fanned ourselves and each other in the dead air, like bees in a hive.

While more lost sheep were brought to the fold, we exchanged anecdotes.

Beside me, one surviving passenger (this was Liang) told of vehicles in motion floating off the road, their drivers still impotently pumping brakes and pounding horns as they flew into their own oncoming headlights.

Behind me, a stripper (this was Estrella) spoke of choking deaths at a drunken party.

An old lady two rows over (this was Colette) said she hadn't felt better in decades. She cradled another who still trembled and wept, having left her mind where her body was found, way in the middle of the air (we never did learn this one's name but called her Chloe).

With relief, I felt myself merge once more into that comfortable composite being, the Crowd. And even the Class, as a balding man in a lab coat, with a nylon stocking over his head, made his way hand over hand along the microphone cord to the pulpit.

"I am Professor Gordon of the Department of Physics. These are Doctor Chandra and Mister Neale." He indicated two other men nearby wearing lab goggles and nose filters: the second and younger held the flashlight and a wild-eyed grin; the first and darker abruptly covered his face with his hands. "I'm here to reassure you with a rational explanation for these recent events." He stretched out his arms toward us, like a blessing.

"The speed of light in a vacuum," he went on, "is a particular and fixed number. Indeed, it is the same number no matter where and when you measure it, which is the basis for Einstein's Special Theory of Relativity, now more than a century old.

"It is an important number, because the rate of every other natural process is bound to it. If it were to suddenly double everywhere, we would never notice, because all our clocks would be running twice as fast, too. It is the pendulum of the Universe; it is the governor of all things—the device that regulates reality's engine."

He was interrupted by the howls of an escaped and receding toddler (this was Danny). After a minute of confusion, we climbed across each other to improvise a human ladder, like army ants bridging a brook in their path, to retrieve the child from the starry ceiling.

"It is a large number," resumed the professor, "but it is not infinite. Our experiment's objective was to make it infinite, in a very small space and for a very short time, before the rest of the Universe could notice. Within that space, we would have achieved the universal catalyst, which quickens all transformations: the *alkahest* of the ancients, the Philosopher's Stone.

"But we … we did not count on the effects of nearby matter … forbidden transitions … quantum tunnelling … The field that was supposed to be only a few atoms across *fed*, like fire, on the free energy of its surroundings. It grew in an instant, like cosmic inflation, to a little less than two kilometres wide before it destabilized—like a bubble that expands until it … stops."

He himself stopped to watch his own clawed hands come together before his face, fingertips touching, as if caging something within.

"We are all now inside that bubble. We are all now living at infinite speed. Eons here may come and go, but, viewed from outside, we and our descendants, and anything we can ever make or do, will have passed too quickly to be seen, gone between one moment and the next.

"There is no way out. Light—and everything else within—is now reflected at its boundary, for the same reason a sunset shines off the surface of a lake, though the water is transparent. But taken to the extreme. Gravity and similar forces do not appear to penetrate because there is now no time for them to take effect."

He lost interest in his hands and let them drift apart again.

"The disturbances at the start came from the redistribution of the atmosphere once its thicker part was no longer held close to the ground. Our other hemisphere, of rock, suddenly released from compression, sprang ponderously away from one side of the bubble to jam into the other."

He cleared his throat then lifted the edge of his stocking and sucked from a water bottle. Frantic whispers flew back and forth among the listeners.

"So that's how things are, and we might as well enjoy them—no, really!" The professor paused a moment, staring into space. "When you think about it—when you really, really think about it—it's not so bad. We're even ... better off this way. Gravity was a tyrant, and I have broken its chains, granting equality to all directions. We 'have slipped the surly bonds of Earth,' as the poem goes, and are now set free—into the Third Dimension!"

From inside his lab coat, he produced two clipboards, one in each hand, then flapped his arms and slowly moved away into the middle air. The flashlight beam followed him.

"Our bones may eventually dissolve from darkness and disuse, and our muscles mostly waste away, but we don't need them anymore. We are becoming a new thing. Here we all are, floating, floating, forever and ever. So many words now meaningless; so much that we've had to worry about in a larger world no longer our concern. No one before has ever been so free, because no one before has ever been so alone."

From the nave's invisible throng, came a sudden rude shout: "God's still with us, Professor Gorgon!"

"Is He, now? Do you hear that, Chandra? My postdoctoral assistant is a Hindu—his God is the essence of the phenomenal cosmos. He told me once he hoped to 'merge his spirit with the stars.' Where will you reincarnate now, Chandra? In an inbred idiot, a hundred years from now? A maggot, in a thousand? A starving bacterium, in ten thousand? And after that, heh, the dead flames, heh, heh …"

Chandra wailed.

"God will do very well without us. Look!" The floating man pointed to the inverted cross beside him, which hung from the ceiling on cables now twisted and loose, its nailed Christ now face to the wall.

"The ghastliest torture machine ever devised by humankind, and the simplest. It was gravity that did all the work, the planet itself pulling at the flesh. To end his suffering, all the victim needed was to annihilate the world. We have done what He dared not; we have put Him out of His misery …"

He curled and spun in mid-air, hugging his knees, convulsing in silent laughter. Then he snapped straight, put away the clipboards, pulled a book from his pocket.

"Hear these prophetic words from the dawning of the Age

of Space — may they be as much a consolation to you as they've been to me. 'The complete absence of gravity,'" he read out, "'will make possible a whole constellation of new sports and games, and transform many existing ones. This final prediction we can make with confidence, if some impatience: weightlessness will open novel and hitherto unsuspected realms of erotica —'"

Right then, we witnessed how the complete absence of gravity made possible the remarkably straight and sure throwing of all sorts of objects. The light was switched off, and order eventually restored.

Over the next few hours, we ninety-two took stock of our resources. Air enough for a millennium. Plenty of water from the slice of frozen canal at one end of our world. Grain for decades, even generations, from the hoppers of a freight train stopped at a nearby siding, then tossed by the earth-shock to snake across the sky.

We proceeded to elect a council (Antonio, Julie, Cheng, Marc, Megan, Mitsuko, and Sam), which then appointed a sheriff — the most senior here of the campus security staff (Gustava). Her first task was to investigate the murder of Professor Gorgon (everyone was calling him that now), found hanged in the abode of the Eternity Machine.

The other end of the braided-wire noose around his stretched and broken neck had been tied to his heels and cinched to bend his body backward into a circle. It girdled in flesh the cable-dreadlocked sphere he'd created, seed and centre of our new reality.

Surrounding the mated pair was a metal confetti of loose parts and tools that stirred again at a touch to bounce off each other and the painted concrete walls of Gorgon's penthouse lab. All here was coated with stagnant water and writhing eels

(Gorgon's tongue protruded like the tail of another), which Biochemistry had been raising for their anaphylactic blood, and which now were loose from their tanks elsewhere in this squat, shared building called the Cube.

The rattled council moved on with its inspection tour. Soon they spotted the killer, cartwheeling through the air. It was the grad student, Neale.

An inquest held by our coroner (Hakim) determined that, after dispatching his supervisor, the young man had taped his flashlight to the rifle from Physics 101 ("Experiment #4: The Velocity of a Bullet") and wired the trigger to his hand. Then he had approached the inviolable Wall, aimed at his reflection, and, counting on the perfect ricochet, shot himself in the head.

A demonstrator to the end, he had pinned two notes to his shirt. One read, "For every action, there is a reaction"; and the other, "Tell them the rest."

Once more, the bell brought us together. Last survivor of the Gorgon trio, Chandra now spoke to us, calmer than before, at first.

"Siddhārtha Gautama, whom we call the Buddha, you see, once said, 'Everything is on fire.' As time passes here, we will grow warmer.

"At first, it will mostly be from the heat of past summers slowly flowing from deep in the rock and out to its cold surface, which is the Second Law of Thermodynamics. Then the heat from our bodies will contribute — it has nowhere else to go, you see. And the same for any fires we make or engines we run, and from rotting and all the other ways that organic substance combines with oxygen and releases chemical energy.

"But after all that has burned, even iron into rust, you see, there are radioactive atoms within the rock — uranium and others — that will release more heat as they gradually turn into lead, et cetera. And, after those are long gone, in billions of billions of billions of billions of years …"

He stopped and stared about, with widening eyes and trembling lip, at the walls, the floor, his audience, his own hand.

"The proton. Every proton in every atom here, you see — to say nothing of the neutrons! — will eventually disintegrate and release a positron that will annihilate an electron — all going to gamma rays, you see."

He spoke louder now so as to be heard over the screams that had, here and there, already begun.

"E equals MC squared, you see, you see, all matter here at last dissolving into a sea of energy, billions of … of degrees, though everywhere the same temperature, final equilibrium, maximum entropy, no movement, no life — the dead flames.

"There is no clock, no clock, you see, that can survive here so long, but … after *our* eternity, the people in the world outside, in *their* next moment, will see, in our place … a great ball of pure radiation, the first moment of such an explosion —

"The biggest H-bomb ever tested — the Soviet *Tsar Bomba* in 1961 — released the energy from only two-point-five kilograms of matter, you see. There are over two billion kilograms in here, of air alone! You see? Our very flesh … the shock wave, the giant crater vomiting ash and poison across the world … not even on the far side of the planet … My parents! My wife! I'm sorry …"

Since he seemed to expect it, we held a trial. The sentence was life imprisonment with no chance of parole, with us his only company. The other two guilty parties had clearly ended as mad as a hatter and a March hare, and for the same reason. Except that the pair found by Alice who fell into Wonderland had trapped themselves in an endless tea time, while for us, it would be forever midnight.

Professor Gorgon had been right in one thing: there seemed nothing left to do but survive.

Our food was sprouts of wheat emerging from their moistened kernels confused but full of hope for light they would never reach. We cranked a dynamo to a small sun lamp for vitamin D; our recourse for vitamin B_{12} does not bear description.

Like sharks, we could not stay still for long without being smothered by our own exhalations. To sleep, we hooked hands or feet into loops along a rope, to be dragged through the motionless air as the one at the end crawled telephone wires from pole to pole, around and around the block.

Except in the sealed stores, moisture was inescapable — our clothes rotted on our skins. Our wastes, for now, and the dead, we collected in plastic garbage bags. Gradually, these and other flotsam drifted like sargasso into a loose pile around the Cube.

We all missed different things: skiing, surfing (both waves and Web), skipping rope, majestic waterfalls, the wind in the trees, the moon at play among the clouds, hot baths, hot food, waltzes, juggling.

With me, it was snakes. As a boy, I'd catch and keep the gentle garters in a glass case in the family cellar, and I'd watch from the dark as they explored their small new world. I kept them a few days at most, a short time even in the short life of a snake, and then I'd let them go and watch as they melted back into the sunlit grass of the field behind our home — a home long since broken, sold, and demolished (ancient history, never mind).

The world may have ended, but we were still a university. The one whose turn it was to bathe in the light would read to the others from a book, and we told each other stories in the dark. Especially popular was a series of courses by Chandra, designed to lead even cleaning ladies and history majors to the frontiers of microcosmology, and to satisfy our morbid hunger for details on how our doom had come to pass.

It was during one such lecture that Chandra finally presented the quadratic formula behind the Eternity Machine. A question came from the surrounding listeners: every second-order equation has two roots, so what was the physical significance of the other one?

Chandra replied, in his usual slow, sad voice, "It would describe the reverse condition, you see, of a volume of space in which the speed of light has been set to zero. From outside, this would appear as a perfectly reflecting and invulnerable sphere that would last forever. And so, obviously, it would be perceptible to the larger Universe, and therefore disallowed in the first place, you see, by the same principles as for the other virtual phenomena we have discussed."

And then, from another direction, "But what if it's not in the larger Universe anymore?"

Chandra was silent for so long that we thought he had slipped away or died. Then he said that it was an excellent question, and he must think more on it, you see, but as he dismissed us, he called over our two engineers (Sami and Francine).

The three conferred excitedly. We, meanwhile, had not stirred — where was there to go? — and others joined us as a new word spread. The council was sent for — it was already here! — and was urgently petitioned for more light, which it immediately granted.

All felt a rush of hope more potent than heroin, but it was with grim faces that the new committee finally put its proposal before the full assembly. Yes, it would be very difficult, but we could construct another Machine to form a new and inverse field just inside the old one, and carry us all, in a heartbeat, across this sad Eternity between one second and the next, and back into Time.

However, it would be impossible to completely exclude air and other matter from between the two fields. Some energy would still be released — much less than before, but still enough to destroy the nearby city and our friends and families there, perhaps all this part of the country. There would be no hope for our own survival.

But Earth would be saved (her innocent serpents, her bright meadows, her spellbound children). And our ashes, at least, will have come home.

We could delay our decision, but the longer we waited, the more corrosion would ruin those parts and materials still available to us.

The proposed plan was feasible, its completion far in the future, and it gave us something to do — we approved it by an overwhelming majority. Soon we were ripping out copper wire from every building, weaving wispy trusses, or scraping narrow tunnels out from the Cube in all directions.

The bulk of the bedrock had already come free of the world-bubble, but we still needed to dig away parts of its edge and to wipe, from the whole face of the englobing mirror, all debris that had come to rest against it. Lasers were built from twisted crystals meticulously grown and cut, along with lenses, prisms, capacitors, and propane-fuelled generators to inject entangled photons into an uninterrupted sheet of light over the entire inner surface.

Time now meant something again — and therefore passed, and therefore eventually began to run out, as we approached the finish. We began to see minor acts of sabotage, then major ones, then assassinations.

There was a war. It was waged with nets and harpoons, forts and dreadnoughts of lashed furniture and living men. There were confused struggles as drifting raids met silent ambushes in pitch darkness, the blind killing the blind. Atrocities happened on both sides. I myself have done terrible things. Our side won. There are few of us left.

I have mentioned few names, I will mention no more. Why list who did what? Can you blame or praise those women — and the men who protected them — who chose their children's lives over yours? Or judge us, who shall see no reward for our labours or our crimes?

And — as has been screamed at me through bloody lips — perhaps it is all for nothing. Perhaps there's been a mistake in the present theory, as there was in the earlier one. Perhaps we have only bought you a few hours, or a few minutes. For the fathers of the first Eternity Machine built and activated it in haste, over the holidays and at night, because they knew at least one other competing group was very, very close behind.

And even if those others are stopped in time — by the echo of this blast, maybe — what of the unlimited future (I mean yours)? From our experience, and Chandra's notes here, you will realize what went wrong the first time and how now to create as small a bubble of eternity as you wish — or as large. Limitless free energy beckons: perhaps, to flee across the light years from the incompetence or insanity of your neighbours, be they a great nation or three men with a spare weekend and a box of tools. It is a very simple experiment, you see.

Well, what I've chosen, I've chosen.

Humanity's writings are now come full circle. Like the first clay tablets of Babylon, I expect that these words, which I've marked on fibreglass-reinforced mud (for I was the recording secretary), will bake into brick in the fire to come (if they are not shattered to dust by the blast even after I've wrapped and buried them deep in further insulation). Well, all these words but one: the next and last.

The moment has been carefully selected so that this slowly rotating mass of stone will be in step when it rejoins the dance of worlds and seasons — if only to match gravitational potentials. Our sufferings near an end — that is, a purpose. I go now to finish my long fall and meet my fate at the focus of a gamma-coloured sky.

__In the token bunker,__ we discuss drawing straws (no tossing of coins, here, or rolling of dice), but there's already one among us who yearns to complete his expiation.

So we others watch him by the status lights as he murmurs beloved names.

Then reaches out and grasps the lever.

And moves it —

Down!

BLISS STREET

CZ Tacks

CZ Tacks *is an Australian writer and artist who is interested in speculative fiction, strange creatures, and collecting more stationery than they can ever realistically use. They are easily identified by their collection of excellent jackets and inability to stop sharing medical history trivia. 'Bliss Street' was the winner of the 2022 Jack Whyte Storyteller Award, judged by Diana Gabaldon for the Surrey International Writers' Conference.*

$\mathcal{B}$LISS STREET

Vanna found out she was a homeowner the same time she found out her dad was dead. The emotions evoked were complex, and she wasn't gonna be the one to deal with them. She tweeted about it instead: *Waiting for someone in your family tree to die and hoping they forgot to cut you out of their will is the only real millennial house-buying strategy.*

Then she threw an overnight bag into the boot of her car, cancelled her bookings, put up a Facebook post saying the tattoo parlour was closed for a few days, and drove to Melbourne to take a look.

There was an evaluation from a real estate agent among the paperwork. It said things like *genuine Edwardian architecture* and *completely untouched* and *a renovator's paradise.* Vanna interpreted this as a polite way of calling the place a real shithole. She'd grown up in the house. It had been a shithole then, and there was no world in which her dad would've improved it.

She arrived on Bliss Street and found that not only had her dad failed to improve things, but he'd also made them significantly worse through abuse and neglect. "Guess we have that in common," she said to the house, picking her way over the broken glass that littered the porch. The wind stirred the dry strings of dead ivy curled around the rusting eave brackets. Vanna decided this meant the house agreed with her.

It was weird to be in the house by herself; weirder still to find that the furniture was gone. The house had been in Ma's family for generations, and so had all the things in it that had been there when Vanna was a kid. She'd known when she left that she was consigning it all to be destroyed or thrown out or sold off by her dad. It was still a shame, though. The only place to sit was a crappy folding chair with sad, thin padding visible through cracking vinyl. Vanna pitched that out the window and into the skip as well.

The door to the second bedroom was closed. Vanna left it that way and went into the master bedroom instead. There, she discovered that her dad had been sleeping on a cot from the army disposal shop, jammed up against the defunct fireplace. The sleeping bag on top smelled so powerfully of sweat and cigarette smoke that Vanna's eyes welled up. She flung it out into the hallway and sat on the cot for a minute, elbows on her knees and head in her hands, until she felt less like she was choking. She wiped her nose on the back of her hand and sniffed hard a few times.

"All right," she said, and stood up. "Let's see what the damage is."

There was a crack in the wall that ran all the way from baseboard to ceiling. Vanna stuck her fingers into it. Even without exerting pressure, the plaster crumbled immediately. Now the crack became a naked stretch of thin wooden slats. The slats, at least, were in good shape.

"Well, that's just great," Vanna said, and went to get a dustpan.

After the long childhood years of moving slow and silent, it felt good to make noise and bang against things. Vanna stomped around with enough force to make the plaster crumble off the walls. It kept on crumbling even after she stopped stomping. She found a fifty-litre white plastic bucket abandoned in a corner. She picked up the biggest chunks and tossed them in the bucket, then swept up the powdery residue and dumped that in too.

It wasn't hard work, but the house was warm and close. The bedroom window, rusted shut, wouldn't move no matter how much she yanked at it. By the time she finished, she was sweating and filthy. The tattoos on her wrist were invisible under the plaster dust.

At least there was the satisfaction of a swept floor and bare walls. The ceiling looked fine, aside from needing a lick of paint.

"House," she said in scandalized tones, "you're naked. Aren't you from the olden times? Showing an ankle would be bad enough, but here you are with it all hanging out."

She glanced out the window. Her dad had even gotten rid of the curtains, but the neighbours' fence stopped her from giving them a show. Besides, Vanna had so many tattoos that someone would have to get pretty close to tell she wasn't wearing clothes once she stripped off her T-shirt and shorts, shaking a rain of plaster into the bucket.

The bathroom had a modern shower head above the antique claw-foot tub, and once it had stopped with the gurgling and the spurts of gross brown water, it had amazing water pressure. Vanna cranked the cold tap all the way up and clambered in without taking off her underwear. The sheer force stripped off the sweat and dirt and probably her epidermis. Someone had left a towel — thin and ratty and full of holes but smelling like laundry detergent — draped over the mirror above the sink. Vanna wiped herself down. Condensation covered the mirror, even though the water had been cold.

Vanna slung the towel around the back of her neck to catch the beads of water dripping down from her hair. She padded out of the bathroom.

Even though it was early afternoon, the house was dark except for the little puddle of light from the open bathroom door. Vanna squinted against the gloom. She dragged a hand over the wall until she found the switch. It moved under her hand, and she made a note to get an electrician in before the house decided to burn itself down, but the lights turned on when she flipped it.

She saw the problem right away: while she was in the shower, the living room window had disappeared.

Vanna went over and rapped her knuckles against the wall, which was now a stretch of mildewed plaster, as if it had never been anything else. She looked over her shoulder. The back door was gone too.

"If you've locked me in here," Vanna said, voice calm against the hot tongue of fear curling around her larynx, "we're going to have a fucking problem, you and I."

The house groaned.

Vanna took two steps into the hallway. By how dark it was, all the other windows had vanished too. She couldn't see the front door; only a pool of darkness where it ought to be.

"You have until I get there to put the door back," Vanna said, and — still wearing nothing but a pair of wet underpants — walked down the hall.

The front door was gone. The plaster crumbled when she touched it.

Vanna's dad always said she was like a rabbit smelling a wolf outside the burrow. It was not a compliment, coming from him; it was also not correct. Vanna didn't freeze when she was afraid. When Vanna was afraid, her instincts screamed at her to fight.

When Vanna's nervous system finally gave up on that particular response, her fingers hurt. A good deal more of the house was missing plaster. The doors and windows were still gone.

At some point between arriving in the house and the doors vanishing, Vanna's phone had died, and her charger was still in her car. So calling for help was out. Not that it had ever been in; she suspected the house wasn't above mysteriously losing network coverage.

Without the window, she couldn't get to the skip, so Vanna filled the plastic bucket with the plaster bits littering the hallway. Then she lay down on the cot for a while and stared at the bedroom ceiling. There was a ceiling rose, its lush curling leaves cast out of plaster, miraculously whole. Once, there had been a pink glass light shade with delicate frilly edges, like a flower unfurling. Now there was only a naked bulb.

"Dad didn't treat you right," she said, "but that's got nothing to do with me."

The house trembled, which might've been a response or the wind or a truck passing in the street.

"What did I ever do?" Vanna said. She was too tired to be angry, but it felt right to make a token effort. "I was—"

Something hot and painful happened in her throat. Vanna swallowed and pressed the heels of her hands into her eyes.

"I was a fucking *kid*," she said.

The house sighed out a long wooden creak.

Vanna gritted her teeth and pushed her tongue against the roof of her mouth. She sat up and wiped her eyes. Her hands were gritty with plaster dust, and the immediate regret was enough to make her get up and go to the kitchen.

She washed her hands and splashed her face and drank from the faucet. One of the cupboards beneath the sink swung open and cracked her right in the shins.

"What the hell was that for?" she demanded, and shoved the door closed with her foot. It opened again, but slower this time, with an apologetic squeaky hinge.

Vanna squatted down and glared at the cupboard. There were a handful of untouched cleaning supplies: rubber gloves, sponges, a spray bottle of something that promised it was *Tough On Mildew!*

"Honey, half your plaster's off," Vanna said. "I don't think this is gonna cut it."

The cupboard door thumped itself against its neighbour.

"Is this what it'll take to get you to let me out of here?" Vanna asked. "Fine. Whatever. I can't wait until I sell you off to some property-flipping weirdo."

She reached for the gloves. The cupboard door slammed shut and she jerked backwards with a yelp, falling on her ass. Her wrist throbbed; the door had clipped it as it closed, right over her honey locust tattoo, and she could already tell she'd have a spectacular bruise later.

"What the fuck," she said, tilting her face up towards the ceiling.

The house didn't answer. When she tried to run her sore wrist under the cold tap, it spat out something black and tarry that smelled like death. When she went to try the bathroom sink, the bathroom door refused to let her in. She kicked the door, which did nothing except make the house rattle with indignation.

"I can't believe you're on Bliss Street," she said. "What a fucking joke. I oughta stick you on a truck and move you to Shitty Childhood Avenue."

There was a spark and a pop, and all the lights went out.

The bucket of crumbled plaster bits she'd left in the hallway had gotten a friend while she was away. Vanna discovered this when she tripped over it in the dark and almost ate shit on the hardwood floors. She caught herself on the wall, which sent more bits of plaster scattering across the floor and took some skin off her palm.

She bit her tongue against the urge to scold the house; she was pretty sure its feelings were already hurt.

The fuse box was near where the front door usually was. Someone had replaced the old-school fuses with safety switches at some point — probably Ma, probably in the mid-nineties by the look of them — so Vanna didn't even have to risk electrocuting herself to get the lights back on. There was a moment where the switch resisted her, leaning into the pad of her thumb, but then it flipped, and Vanna got to see what she had tripped over.

The plaster chunks were dissolving back into thick greyish-white mortar. The second bucket was smaller and filled with loose hair.

If there had been any furniture left in the house, Vanna would've climbed on it.

"Nope!" she said, all but vaulting backwards. "No. Absolutely not." A horrible thought occurred to her, and she added, "That hair had *better not be human.*"

On her next step back, her heel hit something cool and sharp, and she nearly launched herself into the ceiling. When her heart was no longer doing its best to escape her body via her oesophagus, she bent down to see what she'd stumbled over. The house had provided tools. Her heel had hit a plasterer's hawk, and further down the hallway was a trowel. Both looked as old as the house itself, crusted with bits of old mortar.

Vanna looked from the hawk to the bucket and back again.

"No," she said. "Are you serious? I haven't patched up a wall since I moved out." She'd done plenty of it when she lived here. Her dad used to put holes in the wall at the slightest provocation. "Is that what the hair is for? Are we going full historical accuracy here? You know we have other options. Put the door back, and I'll pick up some plasterboard at Bunnings."

The house groaned at her. Vanna sighed.

"Fine, fine. I'll help you put your clothes back on, you enormous slut."

She chose to interpret the sudden hammering of water through the pipes as laughter.

It didn't take too long for Vanna to remember how to plaster a wall. Mortar on the hawk, pick it up with the trowel, push it up the wall, repeat. It would've been relaxing if she weren't very aware of the place the window wasn't. Without it, there was no way to know what time it was. She knew it must've been hours, because she'd finished the walls in the bedroom and was partway down the hall. How many hours? Could it have been days? Would she even notice if it had been? Would she keel over of hunger or thirst or sleep deprivation or mould poisoning and die on the floor of a house with no entry, forever undiscovered?

That was the downside of plastering. Too much time to think.

When she finished with the hallway, she went to the bathroom. The door opened, so the house must've forgiven her. She took a hot shower this time, since her arms and shoulders and back and thighs were all tired in the way that meant they would seriously hurt as soon as she stopped using them. When she emerged, she found that the house had set little sample pots of paint all over the floor in a cheerful selection of white and off-white and yellow. It wasn't enough to paint the whole place, but it had potential. She gathered it up as best she could and lugged it to the bedroom. A pair of ancient hog-hair paintbrushes awaited her on the cot.

Vanna stayed away from the wall where the window wasn't, and instead ran a hand over the wall with a fireplace in it. The plaster was, against all laws of air flow, perfectly dry.

"That's got to be cheating," Vanna said. "Not that I disapprove, mind you, but it's definitely cheating."

She laid out the paints and sat down on the cot, considering.

"I don't work with paints much these days." She gestured at her densely-packed tattoos. "But I'll give it a red-hot go. Did you have something in mind?"

The house didn't say anything. Vanna put her chin in her hands and thought.

Years ago, Ma had shown her a strand of honey locust trees at the edge of the wetlands, dripping with strands of pale flowers. Fractal thorns as long as a child's arm jutted out from the trunks in an impassable tangle. They were weeds, Ma explained, and they were going to be cut down just as soon as they could figure out the best way past the thorns. The thorns were from the days of megafauna, according to Ma. That was why they grew up so much higher than anything trying to eat them could reach. In the lifetime of a plant, ten thousand years without woolly mammoths and ground sloths were the blink of an eye; it remembered, and it kept the thorns.

Vanna had got her first tattoo when she was nineteen: a wreath of honey locust thorns around her wrist. Later, when she finished her apprenticeship and set up her own shop, every client she had asked why she had a crown of thorns on her wrist. She'd spent a couple of lunch breaks adding white flowers and yellow leaves.

She picked up a paintbrush.

"Usually," she said, using the handle to pry the lid off the paint, "the person I'm doing this for gets to pick. They're also better at conversation than you are." She dipped her brush in the paint and paused. "Actually, I take it back. A lot of them are worse at conversation than you."

The mantel was in reasonable shape, so Vanna followed the curve of the fireplace upwards. No sense worrying about symmetry when someone would probably paint over it anyway.

"Do you remember how angry he was when I got my first tattoo?" she asked. She popped open another tin of paint and got another brush going, switching between the two as she worked her way up. "He said all that bullshit about how I could've just stuck him with needles instead if I wanted to hurt him. Said if Ma ever saw it, she'd abandon me again."

More paint. In the absence of a third paintbrush, she dipped her fingers into it and daubed it onto the wall.

"And then he had the temerity, the audacity, the sheer fucking gall to act surprised when I moved out, as if anyone would live with him if they didn't have to——"

She stopped to rub at her eyes with the back of her hand; with only a single light bulb to see by, they'd started to water.

She stopped talking for a while as the painting took shape. Graceful falls of yellow leaves garlanded with pale flowers: honey locust, sans thorns.

"Check it out," she said. "Now we match."

Down the hallway, hinges squealed.

Vanna abandoned the paint and squirmed back into her clothes, in case someone who didn't want to cop an eyeful had opened a door. When she went into the hallway, though, the front and back doors were still missing. The squealing hinges were on the door to the second bedroom, now standing ajar. Vanna hesitated on the threshold. When she brushed her fingers against the door, it swung open smooth and soundless.

Unlike the rest of the house, Vanna's childhood room still had furniture: a narrow bed, a little desk, an empty bookshelf. It was all ruined. The bookshelf was now an empty rectangle sprawled on the floor. The shelves had been ripped out and flung around the room, judging by the dents in the plaster. One of the desk's legs was missing, and the tabletop tilted at a forty-five-degree angle. Only the wall stopped it from slumping all the way to the floor. The bed frame was intact, but the mattress was gone, and someone had taken the time to snap each of the slats in half.

Vanna took a step in, nudging a splintered shelf out of the way with her toes. Dust puffed up at the movement and made her sneeze.

"He just left it like this? For, what, twenty years?"

The floorboards creaked up at her.

There were more problems than the furniture. They became increasingly apparent as Vanna ventured into the room. The floor and ceiling both warped and sagged towards the far wall, a termite's carnival attraction. There was only one crack in the wall, but it was big, a dark horizontal curve like a smirking mouth. It was hard to tell, but Vanna thought the wall might be sagging inwards.

"Does that hurt?" Vanna asked. "I guess it wouldn't. You're a house, you don't have nerve endings. But it can't feel good, can it?"

The house groaned.

"This isn't like the plaster. I can't patch this up."

The door slammed behind her. Vanna bristled, gritted her teeth, counted to five.

"I'm sorry," she said. "I didn't mean what I said before about selling you off. I was upset."

The house was silent. Vanna looked down at her feet. Where the floor sagged, dust had built up like grey snowdrifts.

"This—honey, this looks pretty structural," Vanna said. "I don't know how to fix it, and even if I did, I don't have the tools."

There was a thud. Vanna glanced at the slumping desk and saw a hammer resting where the top of the desk met the wall. The added weight was too much for the desk, which slid down the wall with a bad scraping sound.

"That's not going to cut it. This needs—I don't even know what it needs. A jack, probably. Clamps. Maybe new studs for the walls." She turned in a slow circle, eyeing the damage. "Someone with an engineering degree."

The house was quiet for a while, the only sound the ongoing *scrr-scrr-scrr* of the desk sliding further down. Vanna shifted her weight, and the floor shifted with her. She turned to face the door.

"Listen," she said. "How about this? Put the doors back. Let me go get my charger out of the car. And a change of clothes. I'll make some calls, find someone who can come fix you up."

There was a soft click as the bedroom door swung open.

Vanna didn't run for the door, but it was a near thing. She took two steps towards it and paused when it swung most of the way shut again.

"It's okay," she said. "I came back, didn't I?"

The door eased open with a long rusty rasp. Vanna stepped out into the hallway.

She kept moving slowly as she turned towards where the front door should be. Her knees went wobbly with relief when she saw it, poorly hung and in need of a new lock but present and accounted for. One step. Another. A few more. Her fingers closed around the handle. She tried it. It didn't turn.

"I'll come back," she said. "Can you trust me enough to let me go?"

This time, the handle turned. Vanna opened the door and looked out onto Bliss Street, lit up golden in the afternoon sun.

THE 2023 MAGPIE AWARD FOR POETRY

THE 2023 MAGPIE AWARD FOR POETRY

Magpies are bold and observant, and this year's shortlisted Magpies make fearless observations. As always, many thanks to our judge Renée Sarojini Saklikar, who noted the compelling voice and lyricism of the poems. Here's what she had to say:

Winner: **'octopus boy in winter' by Claire Lawrence**

A beautiful and haunting use of form and repetition with a narrative arc and a strong first-person point of view that retains freshness with nimble imagery.

First Runner-Up: **'How I Earned My Queer Card' by Catherine Lewis**

A fascinating merging of the prose poem with a lyric voice; plus, a powerful witness. We see the speaker in this poem, and they resonate.

Second Runner-Up: **'Perimeters' by Mark Cameron**

Intriguing: an intellect's approach to philosophy, packaged into a poem.

Congratulations to this year's winners, and thank you to everyone who submitted to the contest, including our shortlisted authors: Claire (no last name given), Mark Cameron, Justina Elias, Charlene Kwiatkowski, Claire Lawrence, Catherine Lewis, Jacqueline Pearce, and Tony Peyser.

Claire Lawrence *is a storyteller and mixed-media visual artist based in British Columbia. Her stories and artwork have appeared in numerous publications worldwide and on BBC Radio. Her writing was nominated for the Pushcart Prize and her artwork for Best of the Net. Her goal is to write and publish in all genres and not to inhale too many fumes.*

Chinese Canadian writer **Catherine Lewis'** *debut chapbook* Zipless *(845 Press) was a finalist for the 2021 Bisexual Book Award for Poetry. Her work has been published in* PRISM international, The Humber Literary Review, *and* Plenitude Magazine, *and shortlisted in contests hosted by* The Fiddlehead *and* Room Magazine. *She is a graduate of the Writer's Studio at Simon Fraser University. Her poem 'Golden' was shortlisted for our 2022 Magpie Award for Poetry and appeared in* Pulp Literature *Issue 37. Catch her at catherinewriter.com or on Instagram or Twitter @cat_writes_604.*

Following twenty years in the software industry, **Mark Cameron** *has spent much of the past decade pursuing his passion for the written word. His two novels,* Goodnight Sunshine *(2015) and* 17 Weddings *(2018), were both shortlisted for the Whistler Independent Book Awards. Mark returned to university in mid-life, earning a BA in English and Creative Writing from UBC, where he honed his skills in short prose, poetry, and playwriting. He is currently working toward an MFA in Creative Nonfiction, writing an essay-infused memoir about a year-long camper van trip that he took with his family. Mark is also a member of the poetry editorial board at* PRISM international.

OCTOPUS BOY IN WINTER

BY CLAIRE LAWRENCE

     flakes
         break
a funerary sky
dropping smothering snow
knots of threads
whirling split-plate   bullet-rosettes   dendritic spines

     flakes
         brutal
magnifying the darkness
with light
bleach naked trees
to dead coral

     flakes
         blanket
spools of alfalfa and grass
into barren reefs

flicker the imagination
of our octopus boy
pop-bottle eyes vacillating
to an unmetered beat

    flakes
        blinding
your boy has found a way to see you
said the specialist
in black, grey and colour-absorbing white
his cones and rods replaced
a grim, vatic pronouncement
cancer

    flakes
        alone
short lived
my son has less months
than it took to create him
will he remember gripping
my fiery strands, clinging fussy
or his father's eyes ringed red

    flakes
        kiss
my son's pale skin
cling to eyelashes
he's uninterested
in memories or futures
he wants to build forts   snowmen   angels

flakes
      frosting
tips of tiny fingers
discerning the world with soft intelligence
a day-blind cephalopod
on tentacle touch   sharp smell   florid sense
he's out in moody winter's wildings

flakes
      delight
palm-licking ice
my son present in his playfulness
pushes aside my dream-wishes and crepuscular grief
remember he says
when i was his age

flakes
      short-lived
i must be with him
so i skate in my boots
lob snowballs at the slumbering fallow field
my child has one season
we will play   laugh   rejoice
    until the snow
        melts

How I Earned My Queer Card

BY CATHERINE LEWIS

> *Out of the rain I waited*
> *in a damp parlor ghosted*
> *with little gifts and candy toys*
> *pitting my brain against your will*

'Twilight', Adrienne Rich

As I dance alone in the corner of this packed dyke bar dance floor, my crop top on, my abs out, I wonder what it would be like to not feel left behind, to not be jealous of the avocado-toast millennials who had queer friends to come with tonight, who aren't Gen-X late-blooming sapphics like me. Though I shouldn't bog myself down in definitions, given all these delineations that I've hated. I never expected life to broadside me at way-too-fucking-old-for-this, how I misread the friendly sparkle in your eyes as flirtation, my queer root crush on you forever unrequited, my thirst unsated. *Out of the rain I waited*

and watched your slow fade, never expecting to be perpetually haunted by your electro-toxic combination of brains and beauty.

Sometimes closure is me just pretending to be over something
when I'm not. I slink away, insisting everything's just peachy,
I'm doing fine, my new mnemonic, as if recitation/incantation
could speak itself into truth. Until then, through life I'd coasted,
naïvely never really questioning my Kinsey One status,
just another boring hetero with a teensy hint of never-explored bi.
Promising to not wax poetic, I left my deepest thoughts unposted,
in a damp parlor ghosted

alongside the women I now date, for once we've both swiped
right, I'm too ashamed to admit I'm just a queer newbie, fresh
baby dyke who just got here, still learning the lingo, Lesbian
Lexicon student. Dare not admit I've only seen one and a half
episodes of *The L Word.* Insufficient spine to admit I drink dairy,
that my fridge has no oat milk, almond or coconut, not even soy.
Instead, I earn my queer card by fucking my way into it.
But only this dumb queer newb would be naïve enough to try
wooing her online date, this futchy Converse-and-jeans tomboy,
with little gifts and candy toys

when it would never even cross her mind to get me a card.
At our Christmas dinner for two, as she opens up my pastry
and gadget gifts, the spread of shock across her face
reveals: I've been just a booty call to her, not a person,
never someone she expected to receive a gift from, except for
the way I've spread my legs for her, except for my tongue's skill.
Now forgotten by this girl who took my queer virginity, I cruise
dyke bars, with noctambulant dreams of seducing you, my queer
root crush, wishing that years ago, we hadn't reached a standstill,
pitting my brain against your will.

PERIMETERS

BY MARK CAMERON

Lately it's the space beyond the lights that intrigues me,
amorphous shapes that stand out against a black sky,
little more than perimeters.

I never understood light pollution until that night on
the banks of the Rio Grande, back when my retinas
knew the difference between a satellite and a shooting
star. Funny that it's warmer now than it was then.
Our timing always was a little off.

Tonight, when I told two strangers beside me in that
sweaty little gallery that I was a reader, they congratulated
me. It wasn't until the poets took the stage that I understood.
It wasn't a homonym, exactly. Nor was it a function of the
cochlea, that part of the inner ear that transforms vibrations
into electrical impulses.

Maybe it's Wernicke's fault for hijacking my intentions.
I once read that no two people read the same book. I'm not
sure that any two people hear the same word.

So there I was on the perimeter again, like the freezer-burnt
dregs of vanilla in the rainbow expanse of a Baskin-Robbins
display. And here I am now, watching the darkness from the
deck of this roll-on, roll-off ferry, wondering why I spend
so much time in the shadows when I used to bask in the
glow of the city lights.

PULP Literature

The Bumblebee Flash Fiction Contest
Deadline: 15 February
Prize $300

The Magpie Award for Poetry
Deadline: 15 April
Prize $500

The Hummingbird Flash Fiction Prize
Deadline: 15 June
Prize $300

The Raven Short Story Contest
Deadline: 15 October
Prize $300

Enter today:
pulpliterature.com/contests

THE DRIFT

Jordan Bray

In his work, **Jordan Bray** attempts to reflect the intrigue of the horizon (and grants permission to groan at the pretension). He is drawn to ventures, adventures, and misadventures in strange and interesting places. His art (the drawing part, anyhow) reflects that sentiment. Jordan has been drawing for the better part of thirty-five years but has yet to find that golden balance between passion and profit. Visit him on Instagram @artofjordanbray and follow the story @world_of_the_drift.

168

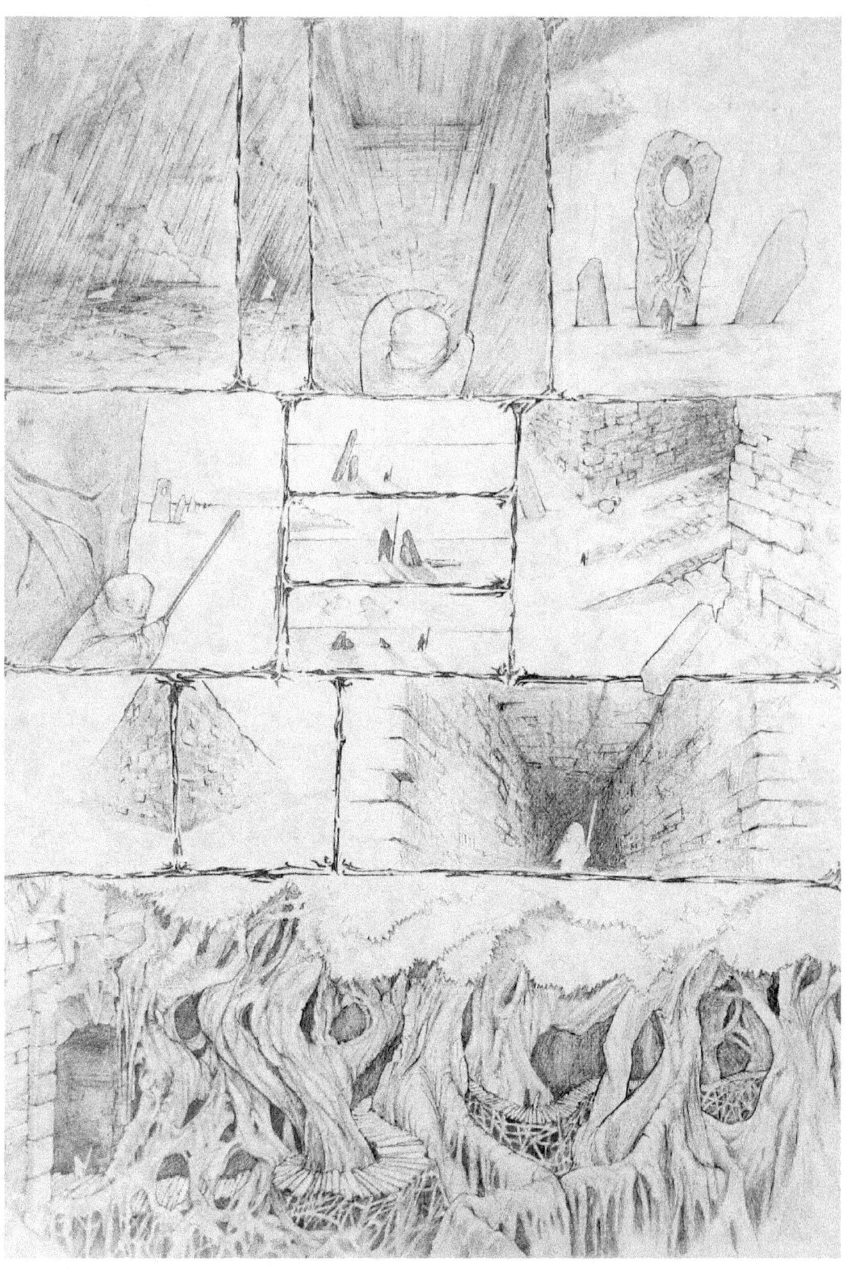

WHERE THE ANGELS WAIT

CC Humphreys

Chris (CC) Humphreys — *born in Toronto, raised in London — has played Hamlet in Calgary and a gladiator in Tunisia, waltzed in London's West End, conned the landlord of the Rovers Return in* Coronation Street, *patrolled the Sun Hill beat in* The Bill, *commanded a starfleet in Andromeda, voiced Salem the cat in the original Sabrina, and played a dead immortal in* Highlander. *He is also a playwright, audiobook narrator, creative writing teacher, and award-winning author of historical fiction and fantasy. He has written twenty-two novels including* The French Executioner, *the Jack Absolute trilogy,* Vlad: The Last Confession, A Place Called Armageddon, Shakespeare's Rebel, Chasing the Wind, *and his recent modern thriller* One London Day. Plague *won the Arthur Ellis Award for Best Crime Novel. His most recent book is the World-War-II thriller* Someday I'll Find You.

©2023, CC Humphreys

Where the Angels Wait

Chris was our first feature author way back in Issue 1, Winter 2014, and he reappeared in these pages with 'The Ankle Bracelet' in Issue 14, Spring 2017. As a bookend to the first ten years of Pulp Literature, *we decided to revisit his first* Pulp Lit *story . . . with a bonus novel excerpt to follow!*

Granada, Andalusia, Spain. August 1986

Sitting on the edge of the bed now, listening. A door opened, shut, someone has come and gone, that much is certain. They've hidden them, and he must find them.

Unless they didn't leave.

"Hello?"

No reply. He has to start. The drawers? Too obvious, but he tries a couple. The cushions? He pulls them off the sofa, feels down the back and side, moves carefully because if they are there, what state might they be in? He finds a crumb-covered coin, nothing else. On the high shelves, then, at the back of the cupboard, rolling in dust? Or in a jar in the bureau, pickled, floating like onions? With others? Alone? Alone, yes, has to be.

He starts to move quicker. Grapes on the table, that's frightening. Eat one? Too risky. Time's nearly up, pull back the sheets, grope under the pillows.

"Who's there?"

He lies back down. "There's no one there," he says, challenging the dark.

He sits up. He knows where they are. His father is in the doorway, making it look small, and he has them exactly where they should be.

"Looking for these?" Dad says, and starts to squeeze his eyeballs from his face.

Off the bed, groping for a light, blundering in an unfamiliar dark to a wall, a door, a switch, filling the room with yellow, running to the window, pulling back the thick curtains. He thrusts his head out into fierce sun and furnace air, and the heat brings him back. He remembers where he is.

It takes him longer to remember why.

6 pm. Jet lag muzzles his head like a warm, wet towel, and he can't figure if home is ahead of Granada or behind. No, behind, it's nine in Vancouver now. Gwen will be getting Sunday breakfast. French toast. Wearing her blue smock to protect her church clothes. If he were there they'd eat, then she'd take the smock off.

"Coming?" she'd ask.

"Nothing to confess," he'd say.

He'll call, catch her before she goes, but after a shower. He wants to make sense when he speaks to her. Before the shower, though . . .

Tom kneels by the bed. He always needs pictures to go with the words. But the only one that comes is his father, another doorway.

Eight years old, pyjama-ed knees to floorboard. He's been there a while. Got to get Dad's face exact, then Mum, then Malk, then Dozy Dog, his white coat and velvet eyes.

His father bursts in. Whiskey breath and showy love.

"You don't need all that nonsense, Tomboy. Only faith you need's in yourself."

Nicotined fingers pulling sheet to chin.

"I pray for you, Daddy. And Mummy and Malk and Dozy Dog. All of us together."

"You pray, then, makes you happy."

"Don't go, Daddy."

"I'm right here, son. Not going anywhere."

Liar.

The shower dribbles on him, making him miss home all the more. Sweat instantly pricking his skin, he dials, and she's there, concern disguised in tales of the last two days, the ordinary worked into comedy. He laughs, missing her. Ten minutes, then he's just hanging on for her voice. Guilt for the waste of money. Guilt for being unable to tell her why he's there. She knows it has to do with his father, needing to go to him dead, as he failed to go three years before when he was dying. Knows it has to do with the dreams; she's held him often enough these last months, shushed his cries, talked him back to bed.

She doesn't know about the eyes.

He hangs up, dresses. He knows where he wants to be for the sunset, has watched it from there twice before. Twenty years ago, the hitchhiker. Ten years ago, the honeymooner, sharing his wandering past with the woman he'd given up wandering for.

In the Albacín, the old Moorish quarter, he loses his way only once on a steep cobbled street among the children skipping rope, the piebald dogs and skinny cats. Soccer commentaries blare from hole-in-the-wall bars. Once, glimpsed behind an oak door ajar, a pocket oasis lures him with blue tiles and cool water dripping from pots of plants and flowers.

Beyond it, though, at the summit, he sees the spire of San Nicholàs.

There's another invitation within its doors, candlelight flicker and incense-laden air. But Tom walks on to El Mirador, the Place of Watching. He's just in time. Across the ravine, the last of the sun burns the walls of the Alhambra fire-red then seeps through levels of pink and bleeds through the single cloud, bruising it from purple to grey.

Others watch, like shades from his past. A young couple in the moment and each other's arms. A backpacker, scraggle-bearded, whip thin, nose to guidebook, already seeking cheap lodgings. It's when Tom turns to leave that he notices the old man crumpled on the patio's parapet, eyes closed and face turned toward the departed sun, a white stick beside him.

Tom takes a step away, and the man's eyelids slide up onto white. He gropes for his stick, swishes it down hard. *"Dinero, por el amor de dios."*

Emptying his pocket into the man's claw hand, Tom hurries away.

Half-sleep, dream-laden. Four-fifteen, hands behind his head, he waits for dawn.

He has what his father called a Spanish breakfast: a plate of churros; a Café Solo, thick and dark; a brandy. Feeling better, he sets out. Granada has changed in twenty years but not that much. Besides, he can see the bullring. According to his map, the hospital is on the other side of it.

The bullring, he thinks, slowing.

Roars, rising and falling, conducted by a red cape and a stick. The matador is young, nervous, but local, so the crowd 'olé' his every pass. The picadors have done their job, gouged their lances deep into the bull's shoulder, his head lower with every run.

Blood, wine, and a searing sun. Dad always insisted on the cheap *sol* tickets, unrelieved by shadows. Tom watches his father raise the wine skin, shooting a red arc into his mouth from near an arm's length. Tom's own ineptitude is clear in the stain on his T-shirt.

The wine skin is offered again, refused. "Had enough?"

"I'll stay to the end."

"Oh, thanks. *Olé!*"

The matador completes his *faena*. A sharp turn jerks the bull around, twists its neck, drops it to its knees. The youth struts away to collect the killing sword while his team goad the exhausted bull to its feet.

Under his breath. "Please, oh Lord, a clean kill, a clean kill."

When it's clean, when the sword drives into that coin-sized hole between the shoulder blades and slips in to the hilt, ending the fight and the bull in an instant, Tom understands. Can share the moment with his father, share Spain. But if it ends dirty, sword skittering down the flank, crowd booing, bull staggering, blood pouring from nose and neck, Tom won't look, and those bluest of eyes will mock him again.

A hush. Red cloth moves under the bull's nose. The sightless eyes are static, filmed over. The bull won't move, so the matador adjusts his stance. Front foot up, he sights along the curling blade. Tom sees the steel wavering and knows what will happen.

The blade slips into muscle, enters an inch, springs out. The bull moves now, and the man leaps beyond the horns as his team circles to confuse the animal, to lower its head for another attempt. Soon the bull will be on its knees again, and there will be nothing left but the short knife at the back of the neck, like pithing a frog in the school lab.

"Dad, let's go."

"It's not over."

"You know it's over. I'm going."

"Fucking go, then."

His father cups his hands, jeering with the crowd.

Rubbing his eyes, refocusing on a grey arch, Tom circles the bullring. Halfway round, white coats appear in a wide marble portico. He crosses over, enters the hospital.

It's cool inside, dark. But it isn't the contrast that makes him feel faint. Nor the smell of hospital, sterile tile, and stone corridor. It's the eyes. Behind the reception desk there's a giant painting. Angels hover near a bearded man who's raising someone from a bed.

But he isn't looking at his patient. He's staring straight out. His gaze tracks Tom across the marble floor. Brown, compassionate, forgiving, loving. The eyes of Christ.

"*Digame?*" The voice is harsh.

"What?"

"*Digame?*"

A woman leans fleshy forearms on her desk, on the plan of the hospital under plastic, condensation where her skin touches. On the instant, his serviceable Spanish is forgotten. Why is he here? What does he want?

"*Habla ingles?*"

"No." She shakes her head, her ears glittering gold.

"*Mi padre ... muerto ... ha muerte ...*"

She raises a finger. "*Momentito.*"

She picks up a phone, presses a number, speaks: death and other words lost in rapid Andaluz.

"*Momentito, Señor.*" She gestures to a bench.

He sits. White coats pass him, suits, a man on crutches. No other patients. Maybe this is an administration building only. Maybe ...

"Good morning, *Señor.* How may I be of service?"

The man is about Tom's age, thick black hair swept back and gleaming in oil. He has spectacles on the end of his nose and peers down them, head back, making him seem older.

Tom holds out his hand. The doctor grips it, holds on longer than formality requires, as if taking his pulse.

"My father died in this hospital, uh, three years ago ... Cancer."

"Yes?"

"There was no ... he was lapsed ... not a religious man. There was no funeral."

"This happens these days, *Señor.*" Under the thin nylon of the doctor's shirt, Tom glimpses a gold cross.

"He … gave his body for medical research."

"Yes?"

There is coldness in the reply, suspicion. Tom hurries on. "I wondered … I need … no, I'd like to know … what became of it? Him? His body?"

Behind them, the clock is loud. Tom glances at it, meets Christ's eyes, looks back.

"Three years? A long time."

"Yes. I …"

The Doctor lifts a hand. "*Señor*, we keep records, we are a teacher hospital. It is most likely that one of the students … you understand? The study, it is … not very nice to a … a not doctor. *Entiende?* You understand?"

Tom nods. If he could lie down he could sleep now. He half turns away.

"Also, there are the transplants?"

Tom feels something in his neck, like a knife pushed in an inch then withdrawn. "Transplants?"

"*Si.* Hearts, lungs, the kidneys, but … you said cancer? So maybe not transplants."

Tom swallows. "Eyes?"

"Eyes?" A shrug. "It is possible, if they were good."

Someone says, "Twenty-twenty even at sixty." Maybe he does.

The doctor smiles, sudden white in the brown face, a flash of gold. "Ah, I see. You wish to know if your father … benefitted, is this the word? Benefitted someone. 'In death there is also life'? Yes? *Entiendo!* This is not so strange. We have families, boys in accidents, mothers who wish to know. The heart beats on, yes?" He nods and takes Tom's arm. "Come, we will look to the records. Then you will be able to sleep, yes?"

Reluctant, eager, now clear, now muzzy, Tom follows. Down the passage lies an answer. He'll leave this hospital, this city, this country. It would be enough. It would have to be enough.

In an office, the doctor rummages in a file cabinet. "Three years. Long time."

He pulls out a folder, goes to the window light, holds the file to himself, head tilted back, peering down his nose, while Tom reads and rereads his own last name scrawled across one corner. The doctor mutters, mouthing words, fingers shuffling papers. Finally he looks up, smiles, and closes the file.

"You can be happy, *Señor*. Your father's eyes were excellent. Because of him a young man, blind for three years, again sees the wonders of God's world."

He is heading back to the file cabinet when Tom blocks him. "May I?"

The doctor flinches, steps around him, replaces the file, slams the drawer shut, locks it, rattles it. "Regrets, *Señor*. Other information is … how do you say this? Secret. No, confidential. Exactly. Confidential." He takes Tom's arm again, not as gently, holds it all the way back to the lobby. Christ beams, the clock ticks. The receptionist's arms make a sucking sound as she lifts them from the plastic.

"And now …"

"Thank you so much, doctor. *Muchas gracias.*"

The smile flashes gold. "*Por nada, señor.*"

The heat makes Tom sway again. There is a cool place he remembers and he heads to it now. Pays the pesetas. Climbs the steps. At the entrance, he looks up at the inscription above.

His Spanish may have all but deserted him, but this he knows by heart.

Give him alms, woman. For there is nothing in life so painful, nothing, as the pain of being blind in Granada.

He enters the Alhambra. It's still early enough that tours haven't yet reached the Generalife, the gardens of the palace. Only a few people stroll the grass paths.

He finds a secluded place, recently watered, drops falling from the leaves of the tree that shades the spot. He lies down.

It's over, he thinks, and closes his eyes. Blue, like his father's. Thank God.

"*Señor! Señor!*" Eyes above him, hazel, angry, pinhole pupils, a hand shaking him roughly by the shoulder. Harsh sunlight behind the figure, Tom shades his eyes, sees a grey work shirt, a lined ochre face. The gardener has a hoe, and he pokes Tom with the butt end. Jabbing him like a picador in the arena. As if he were an animal.

Why? He was doing nothing wrong. This is outrageous.

Tom grabs the hoe, uses the man's resistance to pull himself up. Then he jerks it away, raises it like an axe above his head. He hears someone say, "Leave me alone," then, "I'm not going anywhere."

"Liar!" Tom throws the hoe down at the little man's feet, turns from him, from the voice, from other voices. As he walks away, he sees his hotel room, sees himself packing; the plane to Madrid, the one to Vancouver. Leave Granada, leave Spain, leave …

He goes back to the hotel, drinks two beers, sleeps a little, light and dreamless. Most of the time he lies with his hands behind his head, watching the ancient fan circle, tracing the plaster cracks on the ceiling. He doesn't even try to pray.

Standing in the arch of the bullring again, he checks the time. 10 pm. Two hours he's been there, and though the flow of people from the hospital has slowed, it hasn't ceased. The doctor came out an hour before with a colleague. He heard his laugh, saw gold flash under a street lamp.

No one comes for five minutes. Tom crosses the street. Through the glass door he sees the night porter lay out things on the desk: a Thermos, a thick bread roll, a sports newspaper. Then the man gets up and walks down a corridor. It's opposite the one Tom wants.

Tom crosses the lobby, shoulders braced against a shout. But only Christ watches him. He meets one man who hurries past without a word.

The door to the filing room is unlocked. There are no alarms, nothing hinders him until he comes to the cabinet itself. Pulling out the tire iron he's bought, he jams the flat end into the gap. It slips, catches the second time, there's a moment's resistance, a crack, then the drawer is rushing toward him on nylon runners. He waits a moment, but no one comes, so he flicks his flashlight. He holds it in his mouth, and begins to rifle through the files.

There are very few 'J's. He pulls out his father's file and lays it on the desk.

He does not open it straightaway, just stares at the name. Remembers how he heard the news of his father's illness. How he told himself he was unable to go, how busy he was. How three months later he heard his name called in the hotel lobby in Portland and knew in that instant that it was over. He thinks about the relief he felt, and the guilt in feeling it. About the call to his mother. About how he called Gwen, tried to cry and failed, tried to pray and failed. How there was no funeral, no flowers to be placed, because there was nowhere to place them. He scarcely thought of any of this in three years. Until the dreams began, and now he scarcely thinks of anything else.

The file isn't thick. His father's illness was short, the cancer diagnosed late. Tom backlights the X-rays, seeing the dark shadows covering the lungs. Some scrawled notes, both writing and medical terms impenetrable. A photostat of a death certificate.

The final page is the one he is looking for. He bends to consider. In the end it is easy. There is the word *ojos* followed by the word *azules*.

He laughs. Blue! His father's eyes hadn't been blue! They'd been metal, steel, refracting and reflecting the racing thoughts, only still when they fixed on you for the second before they were off again, seeking distraction, objects to focus his love and hate upon, his hunger boundless for both.

Azules. Opposite the inadequate word is a name.

Tom closes the file, replaces it in the broken cabinet, closes the drawer, stands for a moment with his fingertips on the cool metal. Like the doctor, he now knows who looks at God's world through his father's eyes. And he knows where he lives.

On the other side of the bullring, there's a taxi stand.

"La Cartuja? Cerrado, Señor. Is closed."

Tom drops into the back seat. The driver shrugs, starts the meter. Slipping his hand into the pocket of his coat, Tom grips the tire iron and watches the city slip into suburbs.

With another shrug, the driver takes his money and drives off. Tom stares up at the gates of the monastery of *La Cartuja.* High, crenellated walls gleam in the moonlight and he walks along them, past them onto the street beyond, checking door numbers, then back the other side, ends up at the entrance again. The house number he wants is within the monastery. A sign gives the opening hours for what he remembers is a tourist attraction as well as the centre of the Carthusian order of monks.

The door is oak, iron studded, unbudging. There's no bell. If he knocks, who would come? What would he say when they did?

Tom follows the wall down, comes to a tree, uses it to shimmy up the wall. When he drops down the other side, he lands heavily, his ankle twisting. He falls onto his side, chokes his cry, writhes on the soft earth of a flower bed. It is his ligaments, torn before at soccer, at skiing. He remembers this pain, and how the intensity does, eventually, fade. So he waits, biting his collar. Gets to his feet. The first step is agony. The next a little less.

He limps through a rose garden. It ends in a single-storey structure, the bottom end of a larger building. He passes up the length of it, rattling windows. Finds one ajar, reaches in, slips the catch, hoists himself over the sill. Moonlight pools under the windows, there are dark rectangles on the walls. His flashlight's beam finds a man's face, his eyes on the heavenly host above, smiling despite the axe that evenly cleaves his tonsured head.

The rest of the paintings are similar. Monks in the very moment of their mar-tyrdom, oblivious to the

spears and hatchets of the savages that surround them, their blood pooling under them like moonlight.

The last one depicts a monk just blinded. The savages celebrate, unaware of their real defeat — for above them a host of angels wait to escort the monk's soul to eternal glory.

Tom sweeps the light up and down the canvas. But he cannot find the eyes. Back and forth, up and down. Not a trace.

"Come."

The sound is almost beside him. He jumps, flicking off the light. But it isn't a voice, it's a bell. "Come," it tolls, and Tom now sees figures against lights that spill briefly from opened doors, a man silhouetted for a moment then lost again to the dark. Shapes move past the windows where he crouches to the building ahead, into the chapel itself.

"Come," the bell asks him again.

Through a door into a stone antechamber. Halfway down that room, another door slowly closing. He crosses to it, steps inside just in time. Before him a crowd of backs, brown-swathed, cowls rolled over necks, a couple of suits. "Welcome," the bell says in a longer and deeper knell that hangs above them like a cloud. The monks spread out, kneel. In an empty pew at the back, Tom kneels too.

The chapel sparkles, a thousand candles illuminating white stucco walls, Baroque plasterwork encrusted in silver, statues that seem alive, mother and child, angel and saint. The rich smell of incense makes him giddy. Then a single voice begins to chant, as sonorous as the bell, flowing like rich cream over the company who, in their turn, pick up the single clear line, gently repeat it back. The liturgy calms him, eases his ankle, the struggle of his lungs. He leans forward, places his head onto his hands, and prays. Prayer as dream, a flow of images that come so easily. Gwen, his mother, the Christ from the hospital; he sees each one as they are summoned by a phrase from that clear voice, blessed by each choral reply. Finally, he comes, his father, and there are angels gathered about his head.

Maybe he sleeps, dreamless. Only becomes aware when people are moving past him. But he does not raise his head, and no one speaks to him. The door closes, returning the chapel to silence.

Until the voice comes. The same one that had led the chanting. Speaks above him, as near as a breath. Tom lifts his head to it—and looks into his father's eyes.

Oh, he'd recalled them in dreams. In nightmares he'd seen them plucked from a head, dropped into a jar of formaldehyde. Seen them narrow in fury or enlarge in pain when Tom hurt him, as he'd hurt him in those later years, payment for all those years before. He thought he'd known them. But he'd forgotten their radiance, the lightning flash, northern sky, summer's day wonder of them. All he'd seen in the years since their light went out was the structure, not the substance. And, seeing them now, his own fill, overflow. And as he stands, he lifts the tire iron high above his head, high up where the angels wait.

They take it from him, he lowers his hand, and it meets the monk's hand rising up. Blue mirrors reflect a thousand candles back and forth.

He cannot remember why he's there. Until he does. "Forgive me, Father," he whispers.

The monk smiles, just like Tom remembers. "*Por nada*, my son."

And now for a special treat, we bring you an excerpt from CC Humphreys's classic novel Jack Absolute *(Orion, 2004). We have it on good authority that CC's working on a new novel,* The Resurrection of Jack Absolute, *and we can't wait to read it. In the meantime, here's something to whet your appetite . . .*

JACK ABSOLUTE

The snow lay deep over *Hounslow Heath and the light was failing fast.* They were already late, a double annoyance to Jack Absolute; not only was it considered ungentlemanly to keep people waiting for such an affair, it also meant that by the time the ground had been reached, the Seconds introduced, the area marked out, and the formalities dealt with as to wills and burials, it would be too dark for pistols. It would have to be swords; and by the look of him, his opponent was in fighting trim. If he wasn't twenty years younger than Jack he wasn't far off and, as a serving cavalry officer, would be fencing daily; while it was five years at the least since Jack had fought in such a manner. With a variety of other weapons, to be sure. But a tomahawk or a Mysore punch dagger had a very different feel to them than the delicate touch required for the small sword. Of course, one could only be killed with the point; it had no cutting edge. But the point, as Jack knew all too well, was all that was required.

As his feet slipped yet again on the icy bootprints of those that had preceded him, Jack cursed. *How large will the damned crowd be?* The affair could hardly have been announced more publicly, and many would choose to attend such a fashionable fight. Money would already have been staked. He wondered at the odds. Like an older racehorse, Jack had form. He had 'killed his man' — in fact, in the plural, several more than these gentlemen of London could know about. But his opponent was certainly younger, probably stronger, and above all inflamed with the passion of wronged ardour. He fought for a cause. For love.

And Jack? Jack fought only because he'd been too stupid to avoid the challenge.

He sniffed. To top it all, he suspected he was getting a cold. He wanted to be warm in the snug at King's Coffee House, a pot of mulled ale in his hand. Not slip-sliding his way across a frozen common to maiming or a possible death.

"Is it five or six duels you have fought, Daganoweda?"

Jack, whose eyes had been fixed on the placing of his own feet, now glanced at the speaker's. Their nakedness seemed like vanity, especially as Jack knew his companion had a fine pair of fleece-lined boots back in their rooms in St Giles. However, Até would never pass up such an opportunity to display the superior toughness of the Iroquois Indian. The rest of him would probably have been naked too had Jack not warned him that ladies might attend. The concession had been fawn-skin leggings, beaded and tasselled, and a Chinese silk vest that scarcely concealed his huge chest, nor obscured the tattoos wreathed around his muscles. Midnight-black hair fell in waves to his almost bare shoulders. Just looking at him made Jack shiver all the more and he pulled his cloak even tighter around him.

"Six duels, Atédawenete. As I am sure you well remember. Including the one against you."

"Oh." Até turned to him, his brown eyes afire. "You count a fight against a 'savage', do you? I am honoured."

The Indian made the slightest of bows. Iroquois was a language made for irony. Jack had had too much cognac the night before — the first error in an evening of them — and a duel of wits was one conflict he could live without today. So he reverted to English.

"What is it, Até? Homesick again?"

"I was thinking, brother, that if this young brave kills you — as is very likely since he is half your age and looks twice as vigorous — how then will I buy passage to return to my home across the water, which you have kept me from these eleven years?"

"Don't concern yourself with that, brother. Our friend here will give you the money. It's the least he can do. He owes me after all, don't you, Sherry?"

This last was addressed over his shoulder to the gentleman acting as his First-Second, as the hierarchy of duels had it. The dark-haired young man was struggling to keep pace with his taller companions, his face alternately green and the palest of yellows. The previous evening, Richard Brinsley Sheridan had drunk even more cognac than Jack.

"Ah, money. Jack, yes. Always a wee bit of a problem there." Though he had left Ireland as a boy, a slight native brogue still crept in, especially in moments of exertion. "But, of course, you'll be triumphant today, so the need will not arise. And in the meantime, can you and your fine-looking friend speak more of that marvellous language? I may understand not a word, but the cadences are exquisite."

Jack pulled a large, soiled square of linen from his pocket and blew his nose hard. "Careful, Até, you'll be in one of his plays next. And we all know where that can lead."

The playwright wiped an edge of his cloak across a slick brow, sweating despite the chill. "How many more times can

I apologize? As I said, you were thought dead, and thus your mellifluous name was free to appropriate."

"Well, I may be dead soon enough. So your conscience may not be a bother too much longer," Jack muttered. He had caught sight of movement through a screen of trees ahead.

If the crowd's big enough, he thought, perhaps even the incompetent Watch might have heard of it and turn up to prevent this illegality. Once he would have objected vigorously to any attempt by the authorities to restrict his right to fight. Once … when he was as young as his adversary, perhaps. Now he could only hope that the Magistrates' intelligence had improved.

But no reassuring Watchmen greeted Jack, just two dozen gentlemen in cloaks of brown or green, a few red-coated army officers, and, in the centre of the party, wearing just a shirt, the man who had challenged him—Banastre Tarleton. Jack was again startled by his face. The youth—he could be no more than eighteen—was possessed of an almost feminine beauty, with thickly lashed eyes and chestnut curls failing to be constrained by a pink ribbon. But there was no hint of a lady's fragility in his movements as, laughing, he lunged forward with an imaginary sword.

He looks as if he is on a green about to play a game of cricket, Jack thought, and wondered if it was the cold that made him shrug ever deeper into his cloak. He glanced around the circle of excited faces that turned to him. No women, at least. Not even the cause of this whole affair, that little minx, Elizabeth Farren. The hour was too close to the lighting of the footlights at Drury Lane and her show must go on. Yet how she would have loved playing this scene. The sighs, the sobs wrenched from her troubled—and artfully revealed, carefully highlighted—bosom, as she watched two lovers do battle for her. She would be terribly brave one moment, close to fainting the next.

An actress. He was going to be killed over an actress. It was like one of Sheridan's bloody comedies, not dissimilar to the one in which the playwright had made him the unwitting star. It was an irony perhaps only an Iroquois could fully appreciate. For if Sheridan hadn't used his name in *The Rivals*, if Jack hadn't then felt it necessary to watch some posturing actor play 'him', if he hadn't succumbed, yet again, to the effects of brandy and the actress playing the maid, and if she wasn't already beloved by this brash, stupid, handsome young officer …

Até and Sheridan had moved across to commence the business, and Jack noted the two men with whom his companions were discussing terms. One, an ensign in the resplendent, gold-laced uniform of the Coldstream Guards, was talking loudly and waving his arms about. Yet it was the other, Tarleton's Second-Second, who held Jack's attention. He was standing behind and slightly to the side, his will seemingly focused not on the details of the duel but entirely forward onto Jack, just as it had been the previous night, when his soft whispers had urged Tarleton on. This man had the sober but expensive dress of a rich cleric, the long, pale face of a scholar. And looking now at the man he'd heard named the Count von Schlaben, even in the poor light of a winter sunset, Jack could see that this man desired his death as much as the youth who had challenged him, perhaps even more. And in that moment of recognition, Jack knew that there was more than actresses involved and that honour was only a small part of this affair.

If I am about to die, he thought, looking away and up into the cloud-racked March sky, *the least I can do is to understand why.*

Something had occurred the previous night at the theatre, aside from the play and the challenge. Something that had brought them all here to this snowy common. So it was back to Drury Lane that Jack's mind went, in the few moments before the formalities were settled, and the dying began.

§

Find Jack Absolute *wherever fine books are sold, and watch for* The Resurrection of Jack Absolute, *coming soon from CC Humphreys!*

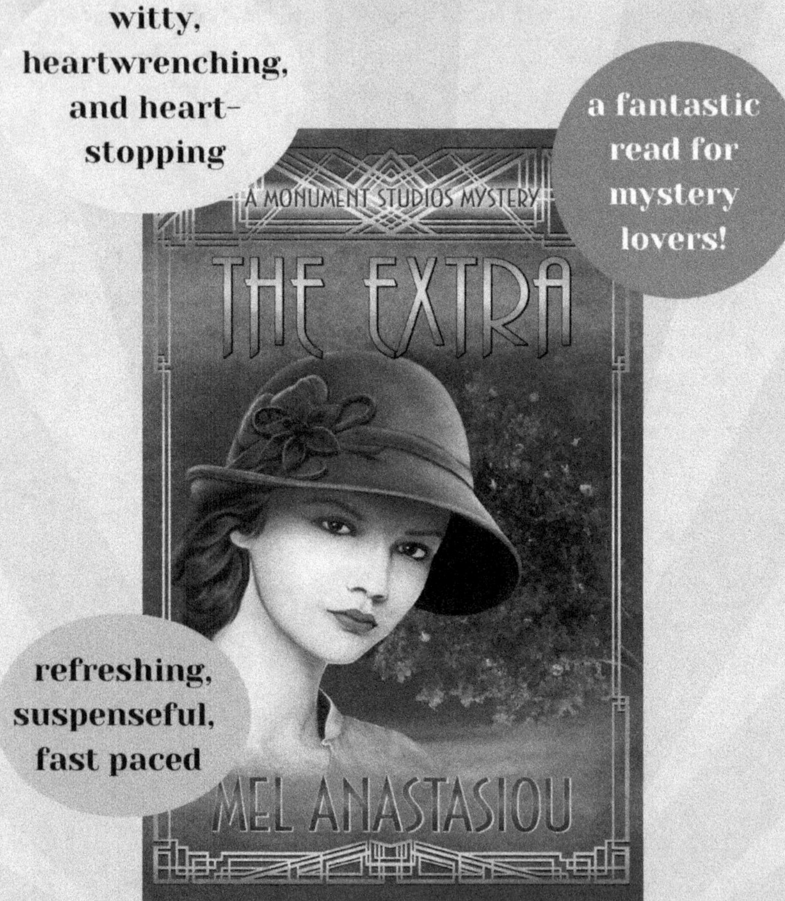
A MONUMENT STUDIOS MYSTERY
THE EXTRA
MEL ANASTASIOU

THE ARTISTS

Tais Teng
Cover artist, American Space Force
American Space Force is Tais Teng's seventh cover for *Pulp Literature*. About this piece, he tells us, "When I heard that Trump wanted a US Space Force, I set out to paint some space marines he most certainly hadn't in mind." In 2 0 2 2, Tais was busy writing a collection of stories set in Zothique, the Dying Earth of Clark Ashton Smith. The book will also have 2 1 of his black-and-white illustrations.

Tais Teng's covers are a combination of digital paintings, HDR photographs, and fractals. In short, he uses whatever works. When he started as an artist, there were no computers, so he still uses paintbrush and pencil. His novel *Phaedra: Alastor 824*, set in the universe of Jack Vance, was recently published by Spatterlight Press.

Jordan Bray
Illustrator, 'The Drift'
Jordan Bray has always sought a place in the career world, where he can immerse himself in creativity. Alas, this world often thrives on chaos and uncertainty, so he busies himself making strange and unique things for the film industry, and for clients who figure, 'Guess it doesn't hurt to ask'.

While travelling in Sydney, Australia, Jordan had a sudden anomalous desire for some visual world building. In his frenzy, he bought a stack of huge paper and a drawing board and, on a threadbare couch in a hostel, drew the first four pages. With no real direction in mind save for a brave protagonist setting off to discover what lies beyond the edge of what he knows, Jordan set out to explore 'what lies beyond *the drift*'.

As this comic grew from a place of escapist wonder into an epic tale, Jordan began to feel the love that comes from the intimate familiarity of a story and its world. He is falling in love with the process of growing, and learning new ways to tell that story. One day, hopefully soon, he can share it with everyone.

Mel Anastasiou
In-house illustrator

Mel Anastasiou loves drawing for *Pulp Literature* because she loves the stories she illustrates. She draws in black and white, working from imagination and inspired by details from Renaissance compositions. You can find illustrations, writing tips, and news about her books and novellas at melanastasiou.wordpress.com, and see more of her artwork on Facebook at Bird and Branch Artwork.

HALL OF FAME

These are the heroes—the Patrons and Pulp Literati whose monthly support helped bring you this issue. Please lift your glasses and give them a rousing cheer!

The Brewers
Robin McGillveray

The Landlords
Dana Tye Rally

The Innkeepers
Ev Bishop
Susan Jackson
Kevin Harris
Gillian Gardiner
Richard Ohnemus
Lorna Erns
Andrea Kepple

The Cicerones
Roger & Anne Anastasiou

The Bartenders
Alana Krider
Richard Gropp
Ron Graves
Dave Wayne
Scott F Gray
Michelle Balfour
Katriona Greenmoor

KT Wagner
Deepthi Atukorala
Margot Spronk
Margaret Elliott
Peter Halasz
Bjarne Hansen
Leny Wagner
Chris Olee
kc dyer
Brighton Hugg
Bryan Moose
Maureen Cooke
K Anastasiou
Mike Sylvester
Katherine Derbyshire
Rapscallion
Shannon Saunders
Megan Shaw
James Carlino
Margot Landels
April DC
Lin & John
 Richardson
Jennifer Getsinger
Finnian Burnett
Anna Belkine

Benjamin Johnson
Suzanne Philip
Fran Scannell

The Regulars
Marta Salek
Rina Piccolo
Jenny Blackford
Akemi Art
BC
Meredith Frazier
Catherine Levinson
Vera
Charity Tahmaseb
Marilyn Holt
David Perlmutter
Paul Anguiano
Adam Fout
Rhea Rose

If you would like to join the ranks of these worthies, you can become a patron on Patreon at patreon.com/pulplit or join the Pulp Literati through our website at pulpliterature.com/join-pulp-literati/.

In search of a writing community?

Join today!

The Federation of BC Writers is here for you!

- ☑ Workshops/ Webinars
- ☑ Contests
- ☑ Readings
- ☑ Articles
- ☑ Networking
- ☑ Discount Membership for for Students and Seniors
- ☑ Digital Writing Circles
- ☑ Find Inspiration & more!

bcwriters.ca/Join

onspec
the canadian magazine of the fantastic

Expect the unexpected.

www.onspec.ca

MARCH 2022
MYSTERY MAGAZINE
All Original Stories

ORNTELLÀDAR
BY A.L. SIRDIS

MARTIN HILL ORTIZ
JAZZ LAWLESS
DIANE A. HADAC
KYLE DECKER
JOHN M. FLOYD
MEHNAZ SAHIBZADA
JOSH TAYLOR
JOHN H. DROMEY

Try our
You-Solve-It
MYSTERY!

The Digest
Enthusiast
Book Fifteen C
January 2022

Tom Brinkmann
Steve Carper
Peter Enfantino
Stephen Jones
Gary Lovisi
Anthony Perconti
Jack Seabrook
David A Sutton

MARKETPLACE

Books

Advent *by Michael Kamakana* • We thought we knew what the aliens wanted. Think again. • pulpliterature.com/advent

Allaigna's Song: Chorale *by JM Landels* • The long-awaited conclusion to the bestselling *Allaigna's Song* trilogy. • pulpliterature.com/allaignas-song

The Extra: A Monument Studios Mystery *by Mel Anastasiou* • Extra Frankie Ray gets her big break on the Silver Screen, until Murder steals the scene. • pulpliterature.com/the-extra

The Labours of Mrs Stella Ryman: Further Fairmount Mysteries *by Mel Anastasiou* • Trapped in a down-at-the-heels care home. You'd be cranky too. • pulpliterature.com/stella-ryman-and-the-fairmount-manor-mysteries

What the Wind Brings *by Matthew Hughes* • Winner of the 2020 Endeavour Award • pulpliterature.com/product-category/novels/matthew-hughes

The Writer's Boon Companion *by Mel Anastasiou* • Thirty Days Towards an Extraordinary Volume • pulpliterature.com/subscribe/the-bookstore

Bookstores

Russell Books • 100-747 Fort St, Victoria, BC • russellbooks.com

Western Sky Books • 2132-2850 Shaughnessy St, Port Coquitlam, BC V3C 6K5 • 604-461-5602 • store.westernskybooks.com

White Dwarf / Dead Write Books • 3715 10th Ave W, Vancouver, BC V6R 2G5 • 604-228-8223 • whitedwarf@deadwrite.com

Conferences & Events

Surrey International Writers' Conference October 2023 • siwc.ca

When Words Collide • August 10–12, 2024 Calgary, AB • whenwordscollide.org

Wine Country Writers' Festival • 28–30 September 2024 winecountrywriters-festival.ca

Writing Resources

Dreamers Creative Writing • Workshops, residencies, contests & more! • www.dreamerswriting.com

Quit the Day Job • A school for writers from Pulp Literature Press pulpliterature.com/quit-the-day-job

The Writers' Lodge on Bowen Island The Muse retreats for writers • pulpliterature.com/calendar-of-events/retreats/

EVENT

36th ANNUAL NON-FICTION CONTEST

INCREASED CASH PRIZES
$1,500 • $1,000 • $500

OCTOBER 15

Non-Fiction Contest winners feature in every volume since 1989 and have received recognition from the Canadian Magazine Awards, National Magazine Awards and Best Canadian Essays. All entries considered for publication. Entry fee of $34.95 includes a one-year subscription. We encourage writers from diverse backgrounds and experience levels to submit their work.

eventmagazine.ca

MAGAZINES

Amazing Stories · Back in print! amazingstories.com

The Digest Enthusiast · Digests past & present plus new genre fiction larquepress.com

EVENT Magazine · Poetry & prose eventmagazine.ca

Geist · Ideas + Culture · Made in Canada · geist.com

Mystery Weekly Magazine · The cutting edge of short mystery fiction www.mysteryweekly.com

Neo-opsis · Canadian magazine of science fiction based in Victoria, BC · neo-opsis.ca

OnSpec · The Canadian magazine of the fantastic · onspecmag.wordpress.com

Polar Borealis · Paying market for new Canadian SF&F writers & artists · polarborealis.ca

Room Magazine · Literature, Art & Feminism since 1975 · roommagazine.com

PRINTING & PUBLISHING

First Choice Books/Victoria Bindery Book printing & binding · graphic design · eBooks · marketing materials 1-800-957-0561 · firstchoicebooks.ca

CONTESTS

Pulp Literature runs four annual contests for poetry, flash fiction, and short stories. For contest guidelines, prizes, and entry fees, see pulpliterature.com/contests.

The Raven Short Story Contest
Contest opens: 1 September 2023
Deadline: 15 October 2023
Winner notified: 15 November 2023
Winner published: Issue 42, Spring 2024
Prize: $300

The Kingfisher Poetry Prize
Contest opens: 1 October 2023
Deadline: 15 November 2023
Winner notified: 15 December 2023
Winner published: Issue 42, Spring 2024
Prize: $300

The Bumblebee Flash Fiction Contest
Contest opens: 1 January 2024
Deadline: 15 February 2024
Winner notified: 15 March 2024
Winner published: Issue 43, Summer 2024
Prize: $300

The Magpie Award for Poetry
Contest opens: 1 March 2024
Deadline: 15 April 2024
Winner notified: 15 May 2024
Winner published: Issue 44, Autumn 2024
Prize: $500

The Hummingbird Flash Fiction Prize
Contest opens: 1 May 2024
Deadline: 15 June 2024
Winner notified: 15 July 2024
Winner published: Issue 45, Winter 2025
Prize: $300

Become a Patron of Pulp Literature

By supporting *Pulp Literature* on Patreon with $2 or more per month, you will be laying the foundation for a secure future for the magazine, as well as ensuring that you never miss an issue! Your subscription includes four big issues of short stories, novellas, poetry, comics, and novel excerpts, delivered to your door or electronic mailbox each year. **Find us at patreon.com/pulplit**

If you prefer to subscribe through our website, go to pulpliterature. com/subscribe.

Or you can send a cheque with the form below to
Subscriptions, Pulp Literature Press, 21955 16 Ave, Langley BC, V2Z 1K5, Canada

Don't miss an issue!

- ❑ **Send me 2 years (8 issues) at the special rate of $90** (save $30)*
- ❑ **Send me 1 year (4 issues) for $50** (save $10)*
- ❑ **Send me 2 years of digital issues for $30** (save $9.92)
- ❑ **Send me 1 year of digital issues for $17.50** (save $2.47)

Name: ____

Address: ____

City: ___________________________ Prov. / State: _________

Postal code: _____________ Country: _____________________

Email: ____

- ❑ Payment enclosed
- ❑ Bill me
- ❑ New
- ❑ Renewal

Make cheques payable in Canadian funds to Pulp Literature Press. Include email address for digital editions and Paypal billing, or subscribe at www.pulpliterature.com.

*for postage outside Canada add $20 per year in North America or $36 per year overseas.

www.ingramcontent.com/pod-product-compliance
Lightning Source LLC
Chambersburg PA
CBHW060412310726
48976CB00003B/1024